PR/

"In a tale of conflicted affections and obsession, of abuse and memory, the past resonates in the present to expose a friendship and explode a marriage with tragic consequences. Complex, masterful storytelling at its best deftly mixing tragedy with courage and ultimately with survival."
JONATHAN SANTLOFER, AUTHOR, *THE LAST MONA LISA*

"Cordelia Biddle has such a gift for storytelling—I was hooked from the first page. This is an engaging, propulsive novel that examines a unique time in American history and will appeal to all kinds of readers."
LIZ MOORE, NEW YORK TIMES BESTSELLING AUTHOR, *LONG, BRIGHT RIVER*

"The unforgettable, can't-put-it-down tale of people who see what they want to see, think what they want to think, and do what they want to do, until, ultimately, their individual paths collide with disastrous results. Mabel Gorne, at the center of it all, is trapped among those who relate to her not as she is, but as they need or want her to be. Caught up in their own mounting resentments and desires, the characters each follow a narrow path between tragedy and farcical comedy. Cordelia Biddle's sharp, dark wit grabs hold and doesn't let go until each of her creations meets its own inevitable—and superbly satisfying—fate. Do not miss this unique and utterly captivating read!"
MERRY JONES, AWARD-WINNING AUTHOR, *CHILD'S PLAY*

"Crystalline storytelling. Biddle, at her best lays a solid narrative foundation then builds us a tale that proves dreamlike. There's enough of the familiar to make it real—small town, midcentury, New England. But the ending, both surprising and inevitable, leaves us astonished in a Gothic wonderland. I thoroughly enjoyed this new novel."
WILLIAM DI CANZIO, AUTHOR, *ALEC*

ABOUT THE AUTHOR

Cordelia Frances Biddle finds inspiration in the connections and correlations within history. Her prior career as a stage and television actress helps her inhabit other lives from earlier eras. She teaches at Drexel University's Pennoni Honors College. She received the 2021 Adjunct Faculty Award for Teaching Excellence.

cordeliafrancesbiddle.net

CORDELIA FRANCES BIDDLE

THEY BELIEVED THEY WERE SAFE

To Lauren,
with love and joy!

11/2/22

for all who have suffered sexual abuse and trauma

"Faith cannot doubt, nor hope despair"
Emily Bronte

NORTH CHESTERFIELD

M abel Gorne arrived among the residents of North Chesterfield like something conjured in a troubling dream. With yellow bangs chopped ruler-straight and gray eyes capable of staring through a person and into a nether universe, she appeared self-enclosed, a person with no history. Whether she chose the effect is difficult to say. The Mabels of this world can be unfathomable, as are the roots of cruelty, or even altruism. Not that she was cruel, despite certain family predilections. But those stories could have been heightened for effect. Mabel was fond of drama.

Descending from the Greyhound bus on that Indian summer day in 1962, she surveyed the Massachusetts village with neither hesitation nor bravado. Instead, she held her suitcase handle as though it were the hand of a fractious child for whom she had little affection. Impatience knifed across her forehead; she looked feral in her isolation. That was one image. Among her future detractors it would become the prevailing impression.

The other and more accepted picture was of a sturdy, farm-raised face, a flat-toned, Midwestern accent and easy smile, all of which made her seem as wholesome as freshly plucked corn. "Salt of the earth" is the term Mrs. Henry Alston used to describe her, as well as other affectionate phrases, slipping them over Mabel's tall shoulders as if the words were comforting arms or a sweet-smelling blanket, an infant's "receiving set"—to borrow another expression from Mrs. Alston's lexicon.

Mabel liked to boast that Ruth White Alston—that proud but diminutive lady was known by both her married and maiden names due to the Whites' long-standing prominence in the Massachusetts town—had come to view her as a surrogate daughter, the child she'd never had. "Ruth White absolutely adores me," she'd say, adding, "Me, of all people. She's just too good to be true!"

Although that scenario is possible, it throws later events into a troublesome morass. Because Ruth White Alston wasn't alone in her grand but faded Victorian home in the elm-lined, residential district of the small college town. She had a husband, a leonine man with a square and prominent chin and a shock of silvery hair. Henry Alston stood a good foot above his tiny wife. Photographs reveal a vigorous, well-proportioned gentleman dressed in one of the dark suits he wore to his dry goods shop down on the town's High Street.

Ruth White was always beside her husband in these pictures, and her white-coiffed head bobbed below his stately shoulders, as if she was all gloss and sheen against a greater and more earth-bound presence. She looked frail, but she was not.

Or so Mabel came to understand during her months of boarding at the Alstons' house and of participating in her hostess's habitual afternoon teas. These were mostly solitary events because Ruth White was strict about whom she considered "suitable" companions for her boarder. The college girls she approved of were society girls with pedigrees and large monthly allowances, who'd been to the opera and Europe, who had beaus at Harvard or Yale or Princeton. These were the elite of the school, the Shetland-cardiganed, tweed-skirted "Mt. Simmons girls" whom everyone idolized and attempted to copy.

Mabel was older than they; she'd already graduated from a hometown university she refused to name and was enrolled at Mt. Simmons in order to do graduate studies in anthropology. Her fantasies of inclusion were just that— fantasies. Imagining herself in camelhair and cashmere coats, stashing away silver flasks of "booze" or smoking cigarettes, and gossiping about necking in public came to naught no matter how often she tried to convince herself that she was the equal of every one of those girls. So she followed her natural impulses, and set herself apart.

Anyone spotting her on the Simmons campus, strolling at a leisurely pace to class, or sitting on one of the rustic benches dotted throughout the campus, would have assumed that this calm creature was someone of enormous worth—the president of the student body, maybe, or the head of the Phi Beta Kappa Society, or the leader of a secret sisterhood of poets. Even her clothing made her seem superior: a fluffy, yellow sweater set and a strand of pinkish glass pearls that were blatantly fake, dime-store beads no one else would have had the courage to wear. The cattiest among the other girls might sniff at those sartorial choices, but she'd always add a caveat: "I bet she's old money. Really old money with some dotty, fabulously wealthy maiden auntie whose family came here on the Mayflower. Mabel's pretending to slum it, but anyone can see she's shamming."

Unaware of the truth, and equally incapable of imagining a more mundane history, the assessment became commonly accepted. Mabel was "unique ... special ... singular," or "*un symbole du raffinement*" to the Francophiles. Within the limestone walls of The Commons, a space that evoked the monkishness of a medieval castle keep, her presence never failed to produce an unspoken drama. The longer she sat, the more frenetic the place became, as though the other students were performing in order to gain her approval. Whether she understood the spell she cast or not, the fact remains that the spell was very real.

The Greyhound bus driver felt it, too, on that day of her arrival in North Chesterfield. "Good luck, Good-looking," he called out just before closing the pneumatic door, and leaving her alone on the sidewalk.

Putting down her suitcase, Mabel awarded him with a smile and a wave filled with bravado and hope.

THE ALSTON HOUSE

By mid-April 1963, Mabel was fully ensconced not only in the Alstons' house but also among an ever-evolving group of freshmen girls who'd begun to cluster around her in The Commons. Mt. Simmons referred to itself as the Eighth of the Seven Sisters (in Simmons' parlance, they were "the lesser Seven Sisters"), and The Commons, despite its name, spoke of exclusivity and rank. Casual mentions of resort homes in Boca Grande or Saranac were a given. Overlooking a manicured greensward, staffed by uniformed waitresses who silently whisked away used cups and saucers, The Commons was devoted to educating the elite, upper-class women in the practices of prestige and etiquette.

Mabel brought her young acolytes there, nonetheless. Most were six years her junior, and the whispers and fawning attitudes of her two or three or sometimes four votaries drew derisive stares from their elders. Those silent rebukes Mabel either didn't notice or ignored. She behaved as if she'd been charged with the girls' tutelage, which, naturally, distanced her from her peers. Their disregard mingled with a kind of jealous self-righteousness, to which she also appeared impervious.

Henry Alston and Ruth White were "marvelously old-school," she might tell the neophytes who had never dared board with strangers, and who regarded her living arrangements as thrillingly audacious. Or, she'd smile and say that she believed "they didn't even know what sex was," a statement that her votaries could only gape at. It was natural at the college for the more experienced young women to lord it over the virgins, to talk openly about going all the way. This chat placed the older girls in a sacrosanct realm, a sort of Mount Olympus of the daring and reckless. Although the youngest assured themselves that they'd wrench off their tartan skirts in two seconds flat if any Eli suggested it, they could no more discuss love-making than fly to the moon. And "sex"—who spoke the word aloud? And in The Commons, right under the waitress's noses!

"Ruth White," Mabel might state, "Ruth White says 'I am a gift from God.' Doesn't that beat all?" Then she'd proceed to describe her latest afternoon in the cedar-shelved attic of Ruth White's immaculate home, and how the two of them had retrieved a box containing a valuable piece of cut glass, or a crate that housed a set of monogrammed cocoa cups bordered in gold. It didn't occur to her that the girls she held enraptured lived in homes where such possessions were commonplace, nor did it occur to the girls to question her wonderment. Instead, they experienced a sense of magic, as if Mabel were converting the quotidian into something pure and rare and new.

"Why, just yesterday, Ruth White showed me a special heirloom. 'This was my great-great Aunt Louisa's. It was brought back from China. Around 1840. It's such fun to share it with the younger generation. Dearest, dearest girl.'

"Isn't that sweet?" Mabel's eyes glittered as she stared though the leaded-glass windowpanes. Uncertain whether tears had produced the sheen or not, her devotees glanced away in embarrassment. Weeping in public was a sin as well as déclassé, as everyone knew. "I mean, isn't it? The Alstons are such dears. So ... oh, I don't know ... so anachronistic. They're always fretting over each other. She bakes him ginger biscuits; you should see the amount of effort that takes.

"And do you know, he brings her a cup of cocoa every night? He creeps downstairs and, well ... I hear him passing my room. Yesterday, she told me I could marry anyone I chose. 'Despite my background'—that's how she put it. 'Despite those old aunties of yours, dear, in Illinois or Indiana, or wherever you come from.' Isn't that marvelously fey? 'Illinois ... or wherever you come from?'"

Then Mabel squeezed the hand of the girl perched nearest to her as if to say they were sisters under the skin. After that, the moment passed, and she returned to another narrative currently consuming her.

That was the extent of each interaction: Mabel talking and the others heeding every word. And they listened, *always*, without questioning, or commenting, or offering the flimsiest of personal reflections, which is why, later, the local municipal authorities were able to reconstruct the story. There were newspaper accounts, of course, but they were so circumspect the reports hardly mattered. According to them, North Chesterfield was a place unsullied where the tawdry or tragic could never exist.

But let us begin at the beginning. A friend of Ruth White, Henry and theirs, Clarissa Tanmere's stories are better told in the order in which they occurred. As is Jim Flaherty's.

THE SECOND FLOOR BATH

From the first month of Mabel Gorne's residence in the Alstons' house, Henry had been a man possessed. The realization had grown, little by little, month by slow, sneaky month, until he'd begun to believe that his body and mind were no longer his own.

It's just that she's so … so youthful … he'd insist silently as dawn after dawn crept into the second-floor bedroom he shared with Ruth White. *So full of vitality. One can't resist a lively personality, now, can one?*

This small stab at candor would flash across his opaline eyes while something larger and hungrier began stalking the edges of his well-formed lips. In the gray morning light of New England, Henry Alston's face would become a welter of conflicting facts.

"Enthusiasm weaves its own peculiar spell," he'd whisper in order not to disturb his wife in her distant and ice-blue, eider-downed bed. "And really, that's the heart of the matter, isn't it? The girl's pure, bounding joy!"

He repeated these fervent invocations daily, and each time he prayed that their meaning would take root. "So young and irrepressible," he'd mumble as he slipped from the covers of his narrow twin bed. "And good-hearted!" he'd add while he walked down the hall to the large, communal bath.

In his proper silk dressing gown, his pajamas and heel-less slippers, Henry Alston would appear entirely reasonable—a man bound for his morning ablutions with nothing more disturbing on his mind than his shaving kit and the business day ahead. Up until the very end, he seemed as rational as the town in which he dwelled.

"That's it!" he'd reiterate morning after North Chesterfield morning. "She's good-hearted!"

Then his daily parade would place him in front of Mabel's bedroom, and he'd pause to listen for sounds creeping under the door. "As well as polite! I can't overlook that asset."

Every day he swore to these and similar phrases. He'd vow them as he shaved and tried to concentrate. Or dressed in one of his dark suits and tightened the knot of an immaculate tie. While he brushed his thick and silvery hair with a pair of military brushes or headed down the wide, uncarpeted front stairs of his wife's ancestral home.

The supplications remained in place while he gave his tiny wife her good morning peck or sipped his breakfast tea. As he warmed his aging Studebaker for the brief journey downtown to his shop on the High Street. While he backed the car from the lilac-lined drive and attempted to set his mind on the workday ahead.

Or unlocked his small emporium's front door and commenced to take stock of the rows of Esterbrook fountain pens, the blue-black bottles of Quink, the boxed sets of lead soldiers and Matchbox cars that lured the town's young boys, and the faux tortoiseshell hairbrushes that intrigued their older sisters.

During each of these activities he'd repeat the same injunctions. "So full of vim. So lively."

He never mentioned Mabel's pale-yellow sweater set or the way the soft, fluffy wool clung to her young and careless breasts. He never mentioned the strand of glass pearls lying discreetly V-shaped on the downy yarn. He never discussed her scent, which reminded him of violets clustering into bloom after a long, hard Massachusetts winter.

He never whispered over her faded lavender nightie or her cotton under drawers dangling on the garden laundry line. He never uttered these words at all, although he thought them. Oh, he thought them.

Night and day, without ceasing, voluptuous images of Mabel rose in his brain. The two of them might be seated in the Studebaker: Mabel on her way to graduate school classes and Henry giving her a lift.

They'd be easing out of the dirt and gravel drive or passing the outskirts of town; they'd be nearing the campus or racing over the jaggedly hilly countryside (Henry liked displaying his driving skills when Mabel sat beside him), and a bit of sweater fluff, a strand as fine and fair as dandelion down, would blow across his nose and settle on his lips.

What a commotion occurred in his thoughts and body then. His tawny face would grow red, and his aftershave-scented neck would thicken; his hands would turn wet with ardor while his eyes saw specks in which Mabel danced. Danced in a damp and clinging lavender nightie, in a white, cotton slip or merely a brassiere and rose-printed panties. Or, God, sometimes she danced in nothing at all!

The vision would leave him gasping for air. His tongue would grow fat while sweat poured from his brow and trickled beneath the shiny, white collar of his starch-filled shirt.

Then the real, rather than the invented, Mabel would intrude, turning to him from the passenger seat. "Are you all right, Mr. Alston? I mean, is there anything I can do? Should we drive toward home and get you some medicine or something?"

He never answered her entreaty. He simply couldn't speak. He'd ease up the car, and buy time by staring at the rear-view mirror.

"Thought I saw something," he might mutter while her voice bounced along with girlish concern.

"Some of that medication Mrs. Alston takes! You know what I mean! The stuff she says is good for her 'peaky heart.'"

The cheerful words would prattle along while a gray-pleated college girl's skirt slid up to reveal a pair of smooth and rosy knees, and the sweater set, the wondrous fuzzy sweater set rose and fell and tightened over Mabel's worried and lovely nipples.

"That medicine stuff… Oh, no, wait a moment. I remember now. She said she keeps a vial of it in the car."

"A minor allergy," Henry would finally mumble, or, "The beginnings of a cold, nothing more. And no, I don't require medication. I never have. I'm as strong as an ox. Always have been." Here his familiar smile would make an appearance, imbuing the words with a private association that Mabel couldn't comprehend.

"Ruth White," he'd continue, "Ruth White may need her little pick-me-up on occasion, but I'm built like a bull."

These words were as close to seduction as Henry dared come, but Mabel remained unfazed. She considered his words endearing in a homespun way.

***

On the morning of May 16, Henry woke as dawn broke the sky. There was no need to glance at the clock on the nightstand; he knew the time without looking. *Five forty-five*, he thought, *the days are getting longer*.

Before Mabel's visit, he had welcomed this change of season. Spring in New England, the "Mud Days" of April followed by the lushness of May, and then a full-fledged and green-spangled June: summer in all its hot and verdant glory. Henry had counted the shifting minutes on the clock with the precision of a meteorologist. He was proud of his far-ranging interests and abilities.

Summer would invariably grow chill, admitting, usually around the Monday set aside as Labor Day, a sudden cold snap that sent vacationers scurrying home and earnest housewives fretting over late-blooming tomato bushes. Then that brief autumnal respite would turn balmy again: Indian Summer with its yellow days and its gathering bees, followed by a true, maple-leafed fall and a gradual graying-down and icing-up of a world succumbing to torpor.

Then winter and the shortest and blackest days of all, when the eiderdown quilts on Henry's bed and on Ruth White's bed had to be augmented with mothball-stored blankets, when the thermometer plunged to zero and below, and the clock at Henry's bedside read 7:30 before dawn broke the sky.

Those reminiscences were pre-Mabel, however. Since the advent of the Alstons' guest, time had played terrible tricks on Henry's body and brain. There was age, yes—always heralded by Ruth White's gratingly cheer-filled warble.

"Well, I declare! I simply cannot imagine how a creature as young as our Mabel could converse with two dinosaurs like ourselves!" Ruth White, in her puffy coif, in her flower-print blouses and tidy skirts, liked to boast that she and Henry reveled in the prospect of their retirement years. Henry, at sixty-three, maintained a frigid silence during these remarks.

But crueler than the reminders of old age, was time itself. To his mind, each day's passage brought him closer to losing Mabel. The seven months of her ever-deepening entanglement with the Alston household would soon spread to eight months. Then eight would give way to nine, and, before you knew it, an entire year would pass, and Mabel and her lavender nightie and furry sweaters would leave.

Leave and return to Indiana or Idaho or some further and inaccessible place where former anthropological students observed the quixotic behavior of Aboriginal peoples cavorting about with stone-age tools. That dire day loomed over Henry's neck like a headhunter's axe.

"Five forty-five," he now repeated under his breath. "Five forty-five. May, the sixteenth."

The words did nothing to diminish the guttural and rhythmic snores emanating from the far side of the Alstons' bedroom; Henry eased one pajama leg from below the covering of sheet and quilt. He did this slowly and with practiced care. Henry took good care of his body, despite his wife's prating about "declining years."

As if she sensed her husband stirring, Ruth White's unladylike snores skipped a beat. In the old days, in the years and months before Mabel's disturbing residence, Henry would have smiled over his genteel wife's vulgar conduct.

Not that she ever confessed to the vice, goodness no! She'd insinuate her husband was dreaming, or suggest the sound was produced by a nearby cat caught in a tree—anything but admit such a low-life flaw as snoring. Not the last White of the great White dynasty of North Chesterfield. Not a family who'd owned both acreage and town buildings since well before that unfortunate upset called the Revolutionary War. Ruth White didn't ascribe to what she deemed "failings of the flesh"—and that included a wide range of activities she'd labeled as "carnal display." There was a reason the Whites had reached the end of their line.

At this moment, now 5:47 by Henry's punctual clock, he wanted to throw a pillow at the lady's superior head. Instead, he stretched his other leg till it slid from the covers. He didn't know where this sudden cruel streak had come from. Never, in all his years as Ruth White's suitor and finally her husband, had he been less than courteous or kind. Never, despite his wife's occasional lapses into disparaging comments on his own less-than-illustrious background, had he been tempted by meanness.

"Mabel," he murmured in a nearly inaudible rush. "It's Mabel's influence." If he hadn't been lying in bed, his square-jawed face would have drooped in remorse. "God," he whispered louder. "Oh, God! What am I going to do?"

He stood up, and reached for the gray silk dressing gown that lay across the ladder-backed chair near his bedstead, slipping it on while he bathed himself in the moon-colored light of morning.

Dressed for all the world to see, for the paper boy or the man delivering milk and eggs, Henry slid his toes into the leather scuffs Ruth White insisted protected her "dear husband" from chill. Then he walked soundlessly toward the second-floor bath.

The upstairs hall was dark and gloomy. It always was, even on the sunniest of days. The tall oak doors and mahogany stair rail, the cherry wood wainscoting and deeply waxed floors were russet-hued and mottled brown-black with years. The colors reminded him of apples left too long in a cellar bushel-basket. The smell was the same, too: slightly sweet, vaguely musky, definitely old.

He padded across a faded green and baize-colored hooked rug that had been a wedding gift from Ruth White's maternal grand-mama, and, again, was struck by the ruined orchard sense of his wife's house—his house now, too. His unquestioning home for close to thirty years. Suddenly everything about the place seemed fallow, antiquated and sad.

By now, he'd reached the bath. The door was ajar; the nightlight still burned, and a faint memory of Mabel's before-bed talcum dusting hovered in the air. Henry breathed in the aroma, imagining himself a speck of the shiny powder as it skittered in the air, arcing over Mabel's bathed and naked body before plunging hungrily to her skin.

Horrible things began happening to his body as he pictured her climbing out of the claw-footed bathtub, a towel in one hand, and her glistening legs straddling the tub's high, porcelain lip. Unspeakable physical urges occurred whenever he indulged in images of Mabel. Besides being shameful, the reactions were also dangerously obvious. Henry glanced at Mabel's door, but it remained thankfully closed.

Then he entered the bathroom, and shut its tall door with gentle but insistent pressure. For an added measure of privacy, he turned the iron key in the latch.

From morning to morning for over seven months, this routine had never varied. Safely ensconced in the locked room, Henry would first flick on the radio near the washstand, allowing the crackling Boston-accented voices just enough leeway to create the smallest hum. He suspected the broadcast concerned the morning news, but he neither knew nor cared. The radio was a ruse. *I'm busily occupied,* the noise said, *I'm a man of the world. I'm attending to affairs of state.*

After the radio, he turned on the hot water tap, letting the steamy brew bubble raucously into the pedestal sink. And then he was ready.

This was the moment Henry most idolized and hated. This was the moment when his muscular knees trembled, when his heart thudded and his ears pounded with blood-soaked clamor. This was the time of the painting.

The painting was merely a framed print, a benign reproduction of a doe-eyed, buxom mother bathing a cherubic and sexless child. The child had golden curls and a wide, trusting smile; and she (or he) was surrounded by mountains of a glowing Turkish towel. The print and its thin, gilt frame hung on the wall that separated Mabel's room from the bath—the wall of Henry's devoted attention.

Sliding the frame on its narrow wire, and swinging the print to one side, a small and nearly invisible crack was exposed. A crack with a hole just large enough for the loving glances of one single eye.

And this was his daily sin-filled indulgence. The activity he castigated himself for. The cause of his disbelieving prayers and bitter reproach. For, beyond the crack and the hole in the wall lay Mabel's enchanted bedroom.

He could see the place clearly. The chest of drawers with its cluttered lace scarf, with its hidden clouds of lingerie, wool socks, nylons and blouses; the wicker chair and the reading lamp; the little desk piled high with all manner of things, with magazines proclaiming the latest fashions, with notepaper purchased from his own proud shop, with bangle bracelets, a comb, the strand of fake pearls and the ravishing yellow sweater set. And finally, Mabel shifting voluptuously in her bed.

"Henry, dear? Knock, Knock! Are you still dawdling away at your morning ablutions? A work day waiteth for no man!" Ruth White's trill caught her husband off-guard. He released the framed print with a sudden bang, causing it to swing wildly on its nail and send a gilded corner into the tender skin above his right eyebrow.

"Damn!" The curse intersected with his wife's resolute cheer.

"What's that, my dear? What did I hear my Henums say?"

"I just cut myself shaving," he lied, then stared ferociously into the mirror. Despite its anger his face had turned ashen and gray.

"On the open medicine cabinet. That's where I cut myself. On the edge of the looking glass, actually." His effort to appease his wife's exacting phraseology was as much habit as anything.

"I said 'darn,'" he lied again.

"Oh, well," Ruth White warbled. "If that's all. A little 'darn' now and then shouldn't be too harmful. But we can't be having naughty language around our young lady."

His wife's words and intonation reminded Henry of butterflies attempting to mate—pretty things locked in a pose of phony passion. Visions of renewed viciousness roared through his brain. He saw himself barging through the bathroom door, knocking the lady flat as he galloped along the hall, vowing revenge for long years wasted and a life of meek acceptance.

"After all the refinements I've been able to teach the dear child. We wouldn't want to see them go to waste, now would we? I do so want to see the darling girl advance in the world. She hasn't had much chance up until now."

"Yes, dear." Henry said the words without forethought, and without attention to their relevance. "Of course, dear."

He looked at the framed print of the mother and grinning child and felt overwhelmed by grief. Time, ill-luck, and happenstance had robbed him of the one glorious hour of his day. He glared at the picture, and then straightened it on its wire. The ferocity of his movement nearly pulled the hooks from the frame.

"I'll be out in a jiffy, dear."

Just at that minute, the object of Henry's devotion and of Ruth White's motherly yearnings shuffled through her bedroom door, sleep still clinging to her naked feet and her yawn and cooing stretch so welcoming Henry could imagine watching it all the way through the dark oak slats of the closed bathroom door.

"Good morning, Mrs. Alston," Mabel half-sighed and half-sang. "Morning, Mr. Alston. I heard you in the bathroom. I heard the radio turn on."

"Mr. Alston didn't wake you, did he dear?" Concern ratcheted upwards through Ruth White's voice.

"No, ma'am," Henry heard, followed by his wife's continuing and anxious solicitude.

"I know a girl your age needs her beauty rest. As well as being bright-eyed for studies."

"Yes'm." Mabel, in the morning, was a girl of few words. Reactions had to be coaxed out of her. "I heard you both. Talking, I mean."

But Ruth White had already moved on, brought to saintliness by Mabel's demure little "Ma'am."

"I'm sure you'll be wanting to use the loo. I know how particular young ladies can be about their appearance. Did you hear that, Henry? Our Mabel's awake. Time to relinquish your secret lair!"

He pictured the entire scene as though he were standing there as well. His wife, small and chatterbox-bright while Mabel towered above. She'd shift drowsily on square-toed feet, shake her moon-round face, and then reach a lazy hand to rub her elbow. And all the while her nightie, her wondrous and threadbare lavender nightie, would stir and shiver, exposing the curve of her inexperienced abdomen and beneath it, a shadowy patch of pale fuzz.

His striped pajama leg stiffened measurably, and his groin grew heavy with longing. *God!* he thought, *not now*. And he gripped the pedestal sink, leaning into its cold porcelain as if temperature alone could staunch his yearning.

"You'll catch your death, dear—with that skimpy thing on." Ruth White's words chirruped through the door. "But then, I've never known a girl so insistent on wearing the barest of clothing!" She giggled nervously here, chagrined beyond measure at the risqué term. "Well, now! I certainly didn't mean bare in that sense! Goodness me, what a silly old thing I've become! I should have said meager or gossamer. 'As on gossamer wings ...' How does that poem go?"

"I don't own a wrapper, Mrs. Alston." Mabel interrupted in her most pragmatic tone.

"Dressing gown, dear," Ruth White corrected with a schoolmarm's murmur. "That's what the nicer folk say. Sofa rather than couch, curtains instead of draperies, we dine as opposed to we eat."

Henry pulled himself away from the sink. The miserable protrusion in his pajama leg had begun to subside. He pulled out his shaving brush and stropped his straight razor, then wriggled his empty pajama fly to make certain everything was returned to normal. *There'll be no more of that vulgar nonsense*, he decided. The disappointment he'd experienced moments before was driven off by tenacious vigilance.

But his wife's continued speech interrupted this injunction. "I know I have no right to lecture you so, dear child, but as we're on the subject of propriety ... Well, how can I put this?" Ruth White grew silent here, and Henry grew silent. Even Mabel ceased her restless stirring.

"Bluntly put, my husband is a man, my dear. An elderly gentleman in your opinion, I realize, but a man nonetheless."

"Oh." Henry heard Mabel sigh, but his wife overrode the noise and the intention she believed had produced it. "Tender ears, I do understand, dear girl! And I sympathize. I do! These discussions of ... well, let us call it human nature. These earthly foibles are never easy subjects to comprehend. But with no other female advice, and with your aunts so distant—"

"That's all right, Mrs. Alston," Mabel interrupted. "I understand. I do." The words were intended to soothe Ruth White, but they had the entirely opposite effect on Henry.

Panic enveloped him. He gripped the sink with his soap-covered hands and leaned against it with all his might. *Oh, Mabel,* he nearly screamed. *What do you know? What have you seen?*

"What I mean to say, my dear," Ruth White was continuing, "I'm sure a girl as pretty as you has had her share of beaus. But such boys as you've had occasion to meet at an all-girls' school like Mt. Simmons ... I don't mean to be disparaging, dear, but boys are quite different creatures than men. What I mean to say is ... well, that little nightdress of yours is very nearly transparent. Why, anyone standing here would see every outline of your lovely young body."

Ruth White's words and Henry's desires collided in an awful rush. He groaned aloud, and his eyes filled with sweat while a giant spasm rocked him from the soles of his feet to the tip of his shopworn fingers. "Are you all right, Henry?" he heard, but he couldn't answer. "Henry, dear?"

Reflexively, he reached for one of his wife's embroidered hand towels and began mopping up the evidence of his passion before it slithered to the green linoleum floor. "A brief cramp in my leg. Dear." He stuffed the towel into his dressing gown pocket.

JIM FLAHERTY'S CAR

The other vital member of Mabel's constellation was Jim Flaherty, who was as unlike Ruth White and Henry Alston as was possible for a resident of North Chesterfield. Nor had those three ever had the opportunity to meet, and why should they? Jim was the town's assistant constable; Ruth White and her husband were models of law-abiding citizens who'd never had so much as a single complaint of an icy or a weed-strewn sidewalk against them. To Ruth White, miscreants, whether children playing pranks on Halloween, or embezzlers in hectic and dangerous Boston, shared a commonality: polite people did not mention them.

How he and Mabel first encountered each other was a mystery neither shared. Not with acquaintances, nor with one another. He could have first noticed her descending from the Boston bus on the day she arrived in September, since one of his duties was to apprise his superior of new visitors. He could have spotted the well-mannered couple with whom she would reside approach her, and then whisk her away to her temporary home. Or he could have seen her strolling through the tall gates at Mt. Simmons, or idling away a Saturday afternoon on the town's High

Street. And Mabel could have as easily seen him at those very same times. Despite hailing from middle America and therefore having a dearth of appropriate courtship skills (as Ruth White believed), Mabel was no naïf. She understood physical attraction, she knew when she'd caught the eye of a boy her age, and she liked the power it gave her. In her personal history, power had been in short supply for females—discounting her authoritarian aunts who ruled only their home—and it had proved a heady discovery at the age of fifteen and sixteen and seventeen. Boys could be dominated; imagine that!

Jim, who had no aspirations beyond becoming head constable at some future date, acquiesced and let her take the lead, although he told himself that he was indulging her. He also came to believe that he was Mabel's shadow image, but because she was enrolled at Simmons whereas his education stopped after the twelfth grade in high school, he knew better than to share that sentiment. If she needed to feel superior, so be it. He understood just how fragile her ego could be.

The later newspaper accounts were fastidiously circumspect when referring to "Under Constable Flaherty and Miss Gorne." He might as well have merely tipped his hat to her once or twice, or noticed her when he drove to the house on the day the unthinkable occurred, and the community all but imploded under the weight of scandal and horror. It was inconceivable that a "townie" should have a friendship, let alone a sexual relationship, with the select of Mt. Simmons: town versus gown being an established social order. No journalist mentioned their many rendezvous, but since Mabel had decided the meetings could take place only in secret, no one knew when they met and where. She'd told him that they needed to adhere to a schedule for their furtive meetings, he because of his employment, and she because of the Alstons.

She claimed she wanted to be worthy of the older couple, but the truth was less noble. Venturing east and entering a school like Mt. Simmons made her feel as if she'd shucked off an earlier and baser life and been reborn. A person like James Flaherty didn't suit the new Mabel. The old Mabel, though, took comfort in his humble origins, because they matched her own. And that was her greatest dilemma: which woman was she? Which persona should she, could she inhabit?

By the spring of 1963, however, she'd begun to chafe under the spell he cast and her own acquiescence, which made her behavior erratic and hurtful. Both of them suffered. She could wound herself as willfully as him.

***

On May 16, they were in the front seat of his parked car. The time was 5:30, or so. Not evening, but no longer fully day, and the sun had already begun to dip toward the western mountains. Looking at the clear and glowing sky, Jim felt an upswelling of hope, but Mabel turned irritable.

"Not here," she insisted. "Jim! I don't want to do it here! Please. Not here!" Thrusting her leg against the passenger door, her tone was petulant and cross, although it was difficult to tell with whom she was most unhappy, herself or the beleaguered Jim.

"Not here! I hate doing it in the car." She tugged at her bunched-up yellow sweater and tried to refasten her lacy, white bra—a purchase she'd made only that morning, and in honor of her clandestine meeting. The brassiere was the most seductive article of clothing she'd ever owned.

"Damn! I can't hook this stupid thing. Why does life have to be so mean?"

Her fingers tingled with strain, and her eyes burned with welling tears. "Damn it all!" The words were an attempt at self-assured worldliness, an attitude she'd witnessed among the bluebloods on Mt. Simmons' campus.

"Damn it, Jim! I'm a mess. I can't go back to the Alstons' house like this! Look at my skirt! I might as well have slept in it for a year! And this brassiere! Why, it's perfectly useless. Good money thrown away for nothing!"

At that moment, nothing in her life seemed fair or even reasonable. Her pleated gray skirt was bunched up and indelibly creased, the bra's extravagant hooks bit into her back, and her lips and cheeks stung from Jim's too-ardent attentions, while the car's damp vinyl interior—shabby on the best of days—stank of cigarettes, steer manure and something bitter like gin. It reminded her of every high school groping she'd experienced, and every run-down family car, memories she was desperate to outrun.

"I thought you were going to drive up to Windsor Haven and get us a hotel room." She wanted him to suffer for his car, suffer for his skimpy education. She wanted him to compare himself unfavorably with the Yale and Harvard boys who strolled Mt. Simmons' ivied quadrangle every weekend. She wanted remorse, apologies and hang-dog sorrow. She also wished that just once he'd tell her to shut up.

In angry silence, she stared out the car's window. From the tangled, bittersweet-entwined woods where his automobile lay hidden, she could see rows and rows of tobacco plants frothing with succulent, new leaves. The leaves stretched upward toward a protective covering of pale beige sacking that made the fields look as if they'd been blanketed by ancient, sun-bleached sheets. In the distance stood twin tobacco sheds, empty at the moment, both of them, gap-slatted, breeze-swept and waiting for the certain harvest. Mabel had begun to despise the sight, which had nothing to do with the quaint New England villages of her Midwestern imagination. But then neither did Jim's wreck of an auto, and neither did an unhooked, crumpled brassiere, or a skirt that looked as if heifers had stomped it.

"You're supposed to be a man. A man with a job and responsibilities. A yearly salary, and people who admire you. You promised to take me up to Windsor Haven. To a hotel with clean sheets and a door that locks. You promised we'd start acting like a real, grown-up couple, and not two lovelorn children!"

"You didn't mind it the first time." The laconic response was delivered as a joke, but the effort fell flat. Silence again engulfed them.

"You told me you liked it then." His broad but vulnerable shoulders shrugged off the line, giving him the appearance of youth imitating age, and doing so badly. He might as well have been eighteen instead of a man of twenty-four. Mabel watched this physical transformation with remorse, but didn't give in. "Told me there was a first time for everything. That's what you said. Them were your very words, lady." His shoulders turned stiff and uncertain while his arms stayed pinned to his sides. He resembled an animal who'd been forbidden to pounce.

"That was a different car." Her cheeks were sore, her lips swollen, and her tears felt dangerously close to falling. "I hate it when you use that backwoods talk," she added through tight teeth. "You sound like you're from Maine."

He ignored the second complaint. "The official car. The official uniform. I guess you wouldn't have done me if I wasn't a cop."

"Constable," she said without thinking, then threw in a desperate, "Don't. Please. Please, Jim."

Both grew silent again. Mabel gave up trying to fasten her bra, and he gave up pretending to be someone else, but they sat as separate from each other as though they'd become strangers on a train. He glared at the car's windshield while she eyed the side window with doleful intensity.

The afternoon was growing dusky, but there remained in the western sky some sense of a world glowing and luminous and bright with mirth—an unseen place of tantalizing possibilities.

The sheet-covered fields of their immediate view, however, the Massachusetts of low-slung tobacco sheds and distant church spires scrabbling through shadowed blue hills, these sights were fading as if the boggy soil of May and its damp evenings were sending up a pall. From a nearby pond, frogs raised a song of passionate plea while a few still-solitary birds made frenzied calls to hopeful mates, throwing their notes into air like gifts no one would ever use. Jim and Mabel took it all in. Neither stirred, and neither spoke. The tension between them was palpable, and as sad as any on earth.

"Sorry, Mabel," he finally admitted.

"Don't call me that," was all she could think to answer. "You know I can't abide that name. Call me Missy." Mabel/Missy hated herself before the words were finished.

"First I've heard you say so ... Missy? For true? Why didn't you say so before?"

"Never mind."

"But if that's what you'd like—"

"I don't. I have no idea why I said I did," she added in a softer voice, but the appeal was fraught with conflict. She and he both knew he couldn't save her from herself; he couldn't change where she'd been born, or where he had. He couldn't help her realize her scattered ambitions, or bring them down to earth.

"The way you sometimes pronounce my name puts me in mind of the Alstons, and you know how hoity-toity those two are." These words were an effort at apology, an attempt to remove him from the older couple's straight-laced category and set him in a spot all his own. But like his earlier failed jest, her reconciliation fell short of its intention.

"Right." The tone and delivery were as flat as mud pies. "Missy."

"When I get my degree, I'm going to insist on Missy. Or, no. I'll use Marion," she continued, hell-bent on self-destruction. "I'll have it written on the diploma, so that wherever I go, I can point to this stupid piece of paper and say, 'You see? This is my name. Marion. Marion Gorne.' And then, when I have my own apartment, I'll frame that dumb, gold-leafed scroll."

"Yeah, well ..." He pulled a pack of cigarettes from his shirt pocket and scrunched the cellophane. "I guess that apartment's nowheres I'd know."

"And please don't smoke," she fairly hissed. "It makes you smell like a chimney. And if I come home doused with cigarette smoke, Mrs. A. will start wondering. You know how demanding she is. And then I'll have to bring you round to the house—and God knows what after that. Tea, I suppose. Tea with that odious crone, Clarissa Tanmere. Ginger biscuits with Ruth White and her bosom-buddy. God!"

"Yeah, well," he repeated, then tried a new tack, stuffing the offending cigarettes into the glove compartment as if he'd made a promise to God. The tragic shoulders became stiffer and the jaw tighter. He didn't look at her at all.

"So how are the old folks?" he added with wounded bravado. "Didja tell 'em yet?" The hated twang was unmistakable. Mabel felt he was rubbing her nose in illiteracy as if it were some kind of tribal endurance test, a rite of passage for which only he knew the qualifications.

"No," she muttered, then clamped her lips shut and twisted on the vinyl seat to stare in his direction. Her eyes were focused and full of agony. *Tell them what?* she demanded silently. *That I'm going to quit their pleasant house, drop my studies without a backward glance, thereby forsaking any and all future careers—and all so that I can marry the assistant town constable? That's what I'm supposed to tell Mr. and Mrs. Alston? That, in a moment of sheer stupidity, I made the most utterly ridiculous promise of my life?*

"I'm waiting for the right time," she finally mumbled, and he read in the terse response everything she hadn't said.

She sighed but didn't speak. She couldn't keep her eyes on his face, and she couldn't allow them to linger on his beautiful neck. It was the back of his neck that had gotten her into trouble in the first place. Standing behind him at the North Chesterfield dime store on the day they'd struck up their first conversation she'd been struck by its utter defenselessness. There was something in its curve that reminded her of a lost child, and she'd been tempted to reach up and stroke the white skin, and give its owner every ounce of kindness she possessed. She hadn't been so foolish as to follow her instincts though, but she also hadn't stared dully at the shop's aging wood floor when he'd turned and looked at her.

"Don't you think you should, Ma—Missy? Tell them, I mean?"

Mabel glanced at his curly hair, defined and compact against the sky and the viney, silent woods. The hair reminded her of miniature bales of red-gold wheat stacked on a hilly field. *If you're born with wavy hair*, she wondered, *does the rest of your personality follow suit? Do you see curves and dips instead of hard, straight lines? Does everything seem easy?*

"I think you should though, Miss, don't you? After all, you can't just walk out the door." His voice was soft and coaxing. As he spoke, he threw a languorous arm over the car's seat until his fingers rested lightly on her shoulder. As if unaware of their movement, the fingers began toying with the yellow sweater.

"Can you walk out?" He laughed. The sound was throaty with suggestion. "Can you?" he repeated. This time the phrase had nothing to do with the Alstons.

"Let's not talk about Mr. and Mrs. Alston now," she murmured. "I didn't weasel my way out of classes to sit in your car and talk." The smile accompanying these words wasn't wholly genuine, but it made her feel better. She hated lies, hated to be boxed in with only falsehoods for answers. She recalled that Mark Twain had written something about truth being easier to remember than lies, but the truth, at the moment, was very tricky.

She wriggled closer to his warm touch and raised one knee onto the car's seat. "I can do anything I want," she said with a boldness she didn't yet feel. "And whenever I want. You know that."

"There's my girl."

She closed her eyes. For a confusing moment the present disappeared, and she saw instead the first time she and Jim had "done" it. "Done" it in the back seat of North Chesterfield's "official" car. And on a "duty" night, to boot. She pictured that raw and blustery late October night all over again, the stars tilting through a cold sky, refracting windshield glass and chrome and leafless branches. She could smell him, too, and feel him beside and then bearing down on her, his wiry hair and the burned-log scent of his "official" jacket, his callused hands tugging at her underpants, and the tremble, like fear, that finally shivered through his body.

"What's wrong?" she'd asked that night. "Why are you shaking? Didn't I ...? Wasn't I ...? Jim ...?" While out of the blue, as if in answer to each unexpressed and unconsidered hope, an owl had begun to call, setting forth a territorial reign and bathing the wintry farmland in a sound as clear as reason.

"You know, Ma—Missy, I really am sorry about that hotel room." The noisy whisper yanked her back into the present while his hand slid down her shoulder to her arm.

"I couldn't get away yesterday. If there was one emergency there were a hundred. Three kittens in trees. An old lady who'd lost her dog …"

His fingers slithered across her chest. "The center of the universe," he said, tapping the bone above her heart. His face was very close, so close she could see the green lights in his pale hazel eyes and the peach-pink line the spring sun had painted below his hairline.

"I don't think so." She smiled. The words, as well as her place in Jim Flaherty's car, began to seem easier—routine, almost.

Mabel decided to avoid decisions for the moment. *They'd wait*, she told herself, as they always did. She remembered her aunts' repeated warning. "No sense in chasing trouble. It'll find you soon enough."

"That's not where you usually say the universe is found." She tossed her chunky blond bangs out of her face. The motion was all the rage on the Simmons campus, but it was new to her and she was now testing its efficacy.

For a moment she imagined matching the risqué pose with a cigarette dangling from one hand and a half-empty glass of scotch and soda clasped in the other.

"Just like a Mt. Simmons girl," she pictured an invented and fabulously wealthy swain murmuring as he bent to rekindle her cigarette with a gold Cartier lighter. She could almost smell the expensive cashmere coat, the silk foulard and the British eau-de-Cologne.

"Oh, you're too kind!" this worldly Mabel would whisper in reply. "I'm really far more prosaic than those other girls."

"Well, you certainly fooled me, Baby!" would be the breathless answer.

She shut off the image with a determined bang. Then she moved practiced fingers over Jim's buttoned-up and decidedly inferior shirt. Windsor Haven, the illicit hotel room, and the secret she'd been withholding from the Alstons began to fade—as did every other fiction in her life.

"You say the center of the universe is another place entirely," she giggled.

"Do I?" he asked while one hand found its way under Mabel's sweater and the other climbed her thigh.

"Yes, you do," she said. She tried to invent further witticisms, but the effort stopped mid-thought.

"Kiss me," she said instead. "Here. On my lips. Kiss me here first."

Then out of nowhere, she added words that surprised them both. "I love you. I love you, Jimmy Flaherty."

TEA

"**D**o come in, Clarissa, dear," Ruth White Alston sang from her habitual chair in the parlor, the pillow-riddled sitting room of her husband's more prosaic parlance. By long practice, her voice carried straight through the pantry and into the kitchen. "You know we don't stand on ceremony here!"

Halting and credulous, Clarissa Tanmere edged her way through the rear "service entry"—as per Ruth White's decree, but paused before treading further into the home. Like everything else about her oldest and closest of friends, the kitchen exuded a faint, self-congratulatory snobbishness. From the china figurines lining the "breakfast nook" to the starched lace curtains over the sink, from the scrubbed surface of the lead-topped "utility" table to the glossy metal of the automatic toaster, all was spic and span with nary a dust mote allowed. The room even smelled like Dutch cleanser, as if kitchens everywhere should learn their lessons here. Cooking, with its messy odors and hedonistic stains, was kept in abeyance in Ruth White's home.

"Cleanliness is next to Godliness ... Home is where the heart is ..." Such were Ruth White shibboleths. "A place for everything, and everything in its place ..." Muttering to herself, Clarissa hesitated one last time on the rag rug near the door to the pantry. Then, "Coming," she called out as she wiped an invisible fleck from her sloppily magenta-ed lips. "I'm coming."

Just as she was about to barge her way through the door though, she noticed that her purple lipstick had smeared the index finger of her right glove. She yanked off the evidence of this inferior social skill and stuffed it into her small beige purse. The cotton glove was too bulky for the time-worn purse, however, and the clasp heaved open flinging lipsticked fingers into the air as if they were cloth snakes leaping from a trick candy tin.

"Clarissa, my dear! Whatever are you doing? The tea will be stone cold before you set foot in the parlor! And I've ginger biscuits, too. Why, they're turning hard as rock crystal before my very eyes!"

"Yes, Ruth White." Clarissa groaned, then shoved gloves and powder puff and lipstick case back into the shabby purse, and wished she could escape the teatime regimen, just this once.

Throughout their long years of school and childhood, the uneven relationship between these two ladies had never altered. The taller and huskier Clarissa had been the first to develop a woman's body; and with the unwanted additions had come greater and greater gangliness and a shyness very nearly strickening. She couldn't help but cross her doughy arms over her budding breasts or stretch her scrawny neck and lengthening jaw down and forward in an attempt to ward off quizzical comments. A braying laugh developed during those difficult years, and her habit of baring her teeth as if she were a horse terrified by thunder.

"Clarissa! You silly thing! What can you be doing still bumping around out there? Certainly not cooking, if I know your habits rightly!" Ruth White's insistent humor startled Clarissa all over again, causing her botched, purple lips to draw back from her gums.

"Coming!" she whinnied while she took one final and pathetic glance at the rear entry door, her exit and only salvation.

"But I'm not a bad cook, Ruth White!" she gurgled as she gathered her wits about her and headed for the parlor. "In fact, it's a hobby I quite enjoy."

"Oh, my dear! My dear!" came the amused answer. "There's that marvelously fey sense of humor that gave your school days such élan!"

Stomping out of the butler's pantry, Clarissa recognized that neither élan nor success nor popularity were words that bore the slightest resemblance to her school years with Ruth White. "Fey" was the only relevant term, but that had been used behind her back, and certainly less often than its crueler fellow adjectives.

"Will Henry be joining us?" she asked, side-stepping her way into the parlor. The tone of her voice changed abruptly with the mention of Henry Alston's name, but Ruth White didn't notice a thing. *Naturally, my oldest friend idolizes my husband*, would have been the response if a stranger had remarked this sudden girlish hopefulness. *Why shouldn't Clarissa adore him? I certainly do. Henry is a perfect gentleman and spouse.*

But Ruth White took no notice of her friend's bashful glances. She hardly saw her stumble into the room. Ruth White's observations were reserved for chintz-covered cushions and needlepoint footstools, for antimacassars gone slightly askew, for moth wings or that despised enemy of all tidy people—the Devil Dust, itself.

"No, dear, Henry won't be joining us today. I believe he had extra work at the shop. Inventory or such. These men, you know, always in a bother about something!"

Here she paused. Not for the world would she purposely harm her childhood friend; chattering about the strivings of the male world would only serve to make Clarissa more uncomfortable about her unmarried state. "Mabel should be home at any moment, however. I believe she was meeting some friends after her classwork. Then we'll make a proper threesome!"

Clarissa's long teeth made a second appearance. *The Girl*, she thought with barely bottled fury. *The Damn Girl.*

In all her sequestered and sheltered life in the town of North Chesterfield, she didn't remember hating anyone as much as *That Damn Girl. The Wicked Wench. The Vile Vixen. The Creature who can prove no true parentage.* Clarissa believed Mabel might be Lucifer Incarnate, but she stopped short of further Biblical references in deference to her father's memory.

Mabel had caused a rift from the first day of her appearance. The pleasant threesome of Ruth White, Henry and Clarissa had been forever sundered by *The Girl's* arrival. There was hardly a teatime she didn't ruin, wafting in late and often dressed in clothes that looked too rumpled for the rag heap.

"Sports today," she'd claim, while Clarissa decided indulging in athletics while clad in a woolen jumper and pleated skirt was the epitome of reckless youth.

Oddly, Ruth White always overlooked these sartorial transgressions. "Now, Mabel, you go give that poor skirt of yours a good ironing," she'd advise. "'A stitch in time,' as my dear mother used to advise. 'We may not walk in luxurious raiment, but at least it is clean and well-pressed.'"

Henry never said anything about Mabel or her clothes, but then men didn't observe these things—or so his wife claimed. It was Clarissa's opinion, however, that Henry's saintly personality not only discerned but disapproved, and that his gracious soul had decided to turn the other cheek. *The Damn Girl* never noticed his magnanimity, which made Clarissa despise her even more.

"So, dear, tell me all the thrilling news in library circles!" Ruth White's words interrupted her friend's reflections, causing the fleshy face to quiver as though it had been caught indulging in impure thoughts. "Did any more naughty children try to borrow that scandalous *Forever Amber*, or have you telephoned their dear mamas, and warned each one about the dangers of bringing vulgarity into the house?" Because of Clarissa's position as the town's head librarian, Ruth White knew every aspect of North Chesterfield's literary gossip.

"In truth, dear, I don't understand why a public institution as revered as ours would make such a purchase. Boston and New York and other heathen places may have readers who enjoy depravity, but our little community should rise above that sorry nonsense."

Clarissa couldn't think of a single answer. Books were books, and if some of the library's adult patrons had peculiar tastes, well, so be it. Let them wallow in shocking language, if they chose. It was her duty to protect only the children. She settled her big feet below her, avoiding both the armchair's ruffled skirt and the flowery footstool poised nearby. The stool looked positively pitiless. Clarissa imagined what its reaction would be if the slightest speck of dirt dared to approach.

"Carnal ... well, carnal ... situations," Ruth White was continuing with a sotto voce giggle, "can be so disconcerting for young minds. Even the merest hint can be disturbing beyond measure."

Clarissa helped herself to a ginger biscuit, but mistakenly eschewed the tiny, gold-rimmed plate. The result was that sugar crystals and crumbs as large as baby peas scuttled all over her broad-hipped lap. She popped what was left of the biscuit into her mouth, and then feared she might begin spluttering dried cookie remnants about the room. She glanced anxiously at Ruth White, but if her friend had witnessed this folly, she kept her observations to herself.

"The young ladies who avail themselves to such questionable fiction need a strong, guiding hand. They believe romance to be, well ... romantic. But in truth, connubial duties are far, far from that ..."

Clarissa wished Ruth White would cease her suggestive chat. It was always the same when she took it into her head to discuss library matters. One thing would lead to another, and before you could say, "Jack Robinson," Ruth White would be going on and on about "carnal situations" and all manner of embarrassing subjects. In fact, it was extraordinarily painful to have "connubial duties" preached in her ears just before Henry entered the room! Sighing, she shifted her ungainly body in the fastidious chair. She felt no different than she had at fourteen; she pictured the rowdy "downtown" boys of her youth staring and whooping and calling her names all over again.

"Men are weak creatures, poor pets, and their failings all too predictable. A desire to over-breed, I suppose. Like cattle or goats or sheep or pigs. The blood, once-roused, creates a response both primitive and foolish."

Clarissa squirmed lower in her seat, and clasped and unclasped her hands. She wished Henry would come home and put an end to Ruth White's prattle, but then had no idea how she'd behave if he suddenly strode into the room. She was sure she'd blush horribly; she always did. And even without this hateful conversation!

"I know I've mentioned this many times before, dear Clarissa, but prior to my nuptial celebration, my dear mother instructed me—"

"What was that, Mrs. Alston?" Mabel's voice took both Clarissa and Ruth White by surprise. Clarissa's hands flew to her face, as though traces of an imagined Henry were still stamped upon her reddening cheeks, while Ruth White exhaled a noisy sigh.

"Oh, my dear!" She involuntarily kicked her dainty feet in the direction of the tea table. The silver tray jittered with the blow, and the porcelain cups and saucers skittered against the filigree spoons. "Nothing, dear!" Ruth White insisted too loudly, then immediately turned her attention to the tea service. "How nice you're home in time. I didn't hear you come in."

Clarissa growled inwardly, eyeing the interloper with the same malevolence a mother hyena employs when watching a lioness approach her young. Her lips twisted back from her teeth, but no smile was present.

True to form, *The Vixen* was wrinkled beyond measure. Her skirt looked as though bears had slept on it, and there was a peculiar odor emanating from her body that smelled at once acrid and as salty as brine.

"Sports?" Clarissa demanded. There was no charm in her voice.

"What?" Mabel asked, plumping herself down beside the tea tray and grabbing a fistful of biscuits.

"I take it Mt. Simmons had athletics today." Clarissa recited the words as if she were talking to a particularly idiotic bank teller. The sound was steely.

"Oh, sports!" Mabel gushed. "Sports at Simmons!"

Clarissa decided *The Damn Girl* was getting stupider by the moment. The realization gave her some pleasure. The final outcome, she promised herself, would be drooling imbecility. "Yes," she stated, "a sporting event. At school."

This pronouncement caused Mabel to descend into loud giggles. Her yellow, fuzz-covered shoulders shook while her creased skirt fluttered over her now exposed knees.

Ruth White misinterpreted the laughter altogether; she smiled as if her home and her good and motherly intentions were the cause of her boarder's outburst. "I'm glad, dear," she intoned with a self-satisfied glance that swept both Mabel and Clarissa into its majestic realm. "I'm glad your university days give you so much pleasure. Youth is a golden time. It shouldn't be wasted."

"No, Mrs. Alston." Mabel's eyes grew suddenly serious as though the advice had slammed its way into her heart. "I realize that." After that she became absolutely quiet; her body ceased moving and her hands and neck and downcast face looked as though they'd been carved from colored glass. Mabel and her secret thoughts might as well have been absent from the room.

Clarissa made no further mention of sporting events. Ruth White posited no more maxims while the mantel clock ticked and then dutifully chimed as it did every day, and presumably long into the future. The horsehair-stuffed sofa and chairs gently sighed under the weight of the three women as the sounds beyond the Alston house, the sparrows twittering in the lilac hedge, the moles snuffling in the lawn, the several cars motoring leisurely home intruded or not depending on each individual listener's ear.

Ruth White surveyed her two guests, a benign smile wreathing her face as she envisioned how she would later regale her husband with anecdotes recounting Mabel's youthful ebullience as well as "dear" Clarissa's too-familiar idiosyncrasies, flightiness being the chief among them.

"But what can you expect, Henums, dear?" she'd add with a pitying shake of her head. "Poor thing, she never married ... And she does spend all her days with books! I never thought it wise to make her a librarian, but her father insisted. Poetry, too! That dissolute Edward Fitzgerald and Lord Byron, and all manner of inappropriate creatures! Well, there you are, Henry! The mind is a delicate commodity." Of Mabel, she would simply coo how right the decision had been to welcome her into their home.

Aware of Ruth White's assessments, if not the specific wording, Clarissa also succumbed to silence, although hers was one of panicky resignation. She stared at the carpeted floor and her square-toed, rain-speckled shoes, listening with an aching heart, and knowing full well that as soon as she heard the Studebaker's tires, she'd be cast into utter confusion by Henry's approach. "Utter darkness," she might have corrected, had she felt the remotest degree of irony, which she didn't. Or, she might have given vent to her wrath, and sent *The Damn Vixen* straight into that unforgiving Hell.

While Mabel, equally mute and immobile, heard only her own thoughts.

What am I going to do? Whatever am I going to do? Oh, Jim. Oh, what have I done?

NIGHT

Henry did return, at the accustomed time and before Clarissa had recited her final "thank-you-so-very-much-for-the-lovely-afternoon-and-tea" to Ruth White. He didn't notice their friend's shortness of breath when he strode through the parlor door any more than his wife noticed it. Clarissa's peculiarities were her own. A maiden lady, they both knew. A maiden lady given to odd flights of fancy and overly original speech. Both Mr. and Mrs. Alston were certain that Clarissa talked to herself, as well.

"Oh, Henry!" Clarissa stammered as he walked into the parlor. "I heard the car approach, but I ..." Here, she began searching wildly for some sensible conclusion to her sentence. She couldn't very well claim not to have recognized the sound of his auto when every hair on her skin had stood upright in frozen anticipation. Nor could she imply that she would have left without greeting the lord and master of the manor. Risen for his entrance, she sank back on the flowered fabric of her chair, but, on second thought, decided to merely perch there as if she had, indeed, been on her way home. "I couldn't have gone without saying a proper how-de-do," she gasped in sorry conclusion.

Ruth White came to her friend's rescue, as she'd done for close to sixty years. When in doubt, that wise lady always reverted to the obvious. It was a trick her mother had taught her and her grandmother before. "Maintain an even keel," she'd been instructed. "Don't splash about, and don't make waves. Invention is for books, and excuses are for fairy tales."

"Henry, my dear!" she chirped. "I'm afraid the tea has gone quite cold."

"There are some biscuits left, though," Mabel added, forcing herself to revive from her slump near the tea table. "Ginger ones. Mrs. Alston knows they're your favorites." She attached an especially winning smile to her words, as if external cheer could banish her miserable thoughts.

Henry watched the smile light across her face. He imagined the expression was meant for him alone, and he felt his heart kick over. "Good," he managed, but that was all. He couldn't lift his eyes from Mabel's radiant face.

Unaware of the many emotions careening about the pillowed parlor, Ruth White murmured in her most flirtatious tone. "You see, my dear. We ladies simply live for your presence."

This unfortunate truth caused poor Clarissa to snort like a frightened colt. To cover the sound, she began to laugh, and the hee-hawing snicker bursting forth from her mouth and nose escalated in tone until she was certain she was about to succumb on the spot. Hysteria and grief seemed to have her by the tail.

"We've been having a very gay time of it, Henry." As she spoke, Ruth White eyed her friend with bitter disapproval.

She'll never learn, Ruth White told herself, *and she won't catch a husband unless she does.* The idea that Clarissa, well past sixty and wholly defined by spinsterhood, by musty books, card catalogs and the stagnant air of a small-town library's shelves, might be capable of change was an issue beyond Ruth White's ken.

"I must run." Clarissa clambered out of her chair, then squinted at her unwound wristwatch. "Goodness! Look at the time!"

"I'll clear the tea things." Mabel leapt up, anxious to be away from the room, from Clarissa's frightened squeals, and from her own panicky fears. The problem of Jim Flaherty would wait. Questions about a career—or the outlandish hope for one—would wait. At the moment, she didn't want to think about anything at all. "I can do the washing up, Mrs. Alston. You just sit." She swept up the tea tray as if it were a laundry basket ready for a garden clothesline.

"I'll help." Henry sprang into action, lunging toward the door just in time to swing it open for Mabel's fleeing figure, and then he flung himself after her. "Wait up. That tray's too heavy for your young hands."

Pulled to her feet as if by a giant magnet, Clarissa rose as Henry vanished, then she tottered near the center of the room, the image of desolation. "I must run," she repeated, but didn't move a muscle. "Lovely tea party." As she spoke, her eyes stayed glued to the closed pantry door. The thing might as well have been the Pearly Gates, a place so remote to her guilt-ridden, Congregational heart that the mere mention of it caused Heaven to rumble and all the saints to roar. She draped her purse handle over her wrist as if collecting her wits and her reason. "I didn't realize it was so late."

***

Alone in the kitchen with Mabel, Henry believed himself transported. The electric ceiling lamp seemed to suffuse the place with a brilliant glow. Golden halos appeared to float back and forth between the automatic toaster and the cookery stove, past the wet sink and the washboard, over the breakfast nook chairs and the icebox door, gracing them all with religious light.

"Mabel," Henry whispered beneath his breath to the girl's lovely back. "Mabel, my dear."

Milky white steam billowed lazily around her elbows and shoulders, as if she, like the simple room, had been transformed. She might have been a goddess or a sprite, something with gauzy wings and an all-forgiving mind.

"Mabel," he ventured louder, while Mabel, lost in her apprehensions about Jim Flaherty and graduate studies at Simmons College, finally heard her name above the swish of soapsuds and the plink of china slipping into the sink.

"Yes, Mr. Alston?" She turned toward him with what she considered to be her most reasonable expression. "It's nice of you to offer to help me," she said, though in truth Henry was doing nothing but standing there.

"It's nice to have you in the house." The words seemed remarkably daring. In the space of two or three seconds, he invented all sorts of wondrous responses falling from her lips.

I love being here, she might murmur, adding, *with you* in a sultry giggle. Then, ever practical, she'd hurry to include

56

a passionately whispered: *Will you drive me to school tomorrow, so that we can... talk?* The word "talk" would be heavy with meaning.

Instead, she uttered a breezy, "Thanks," before retreating into herself. Her eyes grew a darker gray; trouble welled in them, followed by something primitive, like fear. She was clearly wrestling with some awesome, private demon, and Henry watched the girl of his dreams turn her voluptuous and healthy body into something terrified and weak. Every ounce of strength seemed to desert her.

"I like this house, too," she tacked on. The addition might have been made out of duty, but he prayed that it was not.

Hoping for the impossible, he misread every one of Mabel's signs. He assumed the anguish confronting her was her own awakening ardor, and that she'd soon grow to worship him as much as he idolized her. While Mabel, regarding his stolid, gray-suited figure, decided that he was the most stalwart, kind and noble friend a person could have.

"Ever since I arrived," she continued with some effort, "you've been so awfully good to me. Réally wonderful ... And I ... and I ..."

Henry heard each moment's hesitation. Part of him wanted to stop the painful confession, take her in his arms and explain that what she felt was reciprocated in full. The other half doted on her abject confusion. He felt himself growing bolder and manlier by the moment.

"Because I was so lost, I guess ... coming here ... well, to New England for the first time, and Mt. Simmons, and I didn't know anyone, didn't have any friends ... and you ... you both ..."

The "both" surprised him, but only momentarily. Naturally, she would say that, he assured himself. She's in Ruth White's kitchen, after all. It's merely part of her exquisite delicacy of sentiment. She can't be as forthright as she wants. She knows she has to bide her time.

"And I feel so terrible about all this. I do. I do!" Mabel was very near tears at this point. "But I just don't think I have another choice!"

The oblique utterances made perfect sense to Mabel; she understood who and what she was discussing, after all. As did Henry. Except that his perceptions were wrong.

He watched her down-colored breasts heave with worry, and her steam-dampened face quiver with incipient sobs. Tiny beads of moisture played across her flushed cheekbones and sorrowful lips. He decided he'd never seen a picture more succulent. He imagined licking every inch of Mabel's face, and then drifting farther. It required all his concentration to remain where he was and keep his hands attached to the dishtowel.

"Of course, that's silly, isn't it, Mr. Alston? I do have a choice. I mean, we all have choice. Life isn't pre-ordained, is it? Even if we've made foolish promises or ... or committed ourselves to something we don't whole-heartedly believe ... or had some difficult experiences. It's not too late to make a change, is it? I mean, it's never too late. You believe that, too, don't you?"

Henry had never heard her so communicative. In all their months together, her few words had been augmented by massive and emotion-packed silence that he'd been forced to translate, finding words for the feelings she was too shy to express. Now, it seemed as if she were speaking for both of them.

"I understand, my dear. I understand everything."

"Oh, you're so good! I just knew you would!" And she was about to fling herself toward her savior's neck when Ruth White marched through the door.

The tiny lady's arrival startled Henry horribly, but it disturbed Mabel more. She understood that mentioning a would-be suitor like James Flaherty would meet with gigantic disapproval, that before she could arrive at the core of her problem she would have to navigate through a sea of hyper-critical questions.

"He's a what?" she could almost hear Mrs. Alston demand, followed by, "Where did you meet this stellar youth?" And then, the sharpest cut of all: "I suppose you've kept your dear, distant aunts equally in the dark." The judgment passed on Mabel's family would turn each one into a bovine and senseless creature.

She drew back from the anticipated lecture, and Henry drew back from his own interrupted hopes while Ruth White, intent on the idea that had driven her into the kitchen, shook her head in both despair and frustration.

"Poor, poor thing! Clarissa is greatly to be pitied! Never married! And never will be, either! Not if she continues in that positively self-involved manner. Really, I've never seen a person so determined to defeat herself. And my closest friend, on top of it! My dearest friend in the world!

"Well, it's her father's fault—may he rest in peace. Her father's fault entirely. But then he didn't have very easy clay to mold when it came to Clarissa. A career! Of all the pig-headed and senseless folly."

The words attacked Mabel's brain as if each had been studded with flaying knives.

***

When all had been tucked away, dinner served and cleaned up and the house returned to its spotless order, when Ruth White had been ensconced in her blue-pillowed bed, and her nightly libation of warm cocoa carried from the kitchen, when the worlds both without and within the Alstons' tidy walls seemed so peaceful and secure that even the parlor clock tick-tocked an uninterrupted measure up the waxed front stairs, Mabel slipped into the second floor bathroom.

She'd waited for the moment, pretending patience she didn't feel, existing in the ruined skirt and rumpled sweater set all during the interminable teatime and equally painful dinner hour. The odors of Jim Flaherty's needs and her own acquiescence had surrounded her every move, but she'd remained unwashed and untidied and as if doing a form of penance.

"Rub its face in it," she heard the invisible voices of her two aunts bark in unison. "That's the only way it's going to learn." The order had been directed at a new hound puppy and its unhappy encounter with a braided rug, but she felt the warning could apply to herself as easily.

"Then throw the wretched creature outside. Never mind the whimpers. The damn thing's got to learn some manners."

She unlaced the brown and white saddle shoes that had been scuffed by Jim's leather boots, pulled off the white socks that were smudged by his muddy soles, unzipped the ruined, pleated skirt and unbuttoned the rumpled sweater set. The yellow wool looked as useless as husked corn silk left wilting in the sun. She flung the clothes, one by one, onto the bathroom floor.

Nothing had remained untouched during her secret encounter. Jim's presence was everywhere. Even her half-slip bore the clammy marks of his hand print, and her lacy, white brassiere looked totally spent, as if its flimsy expanse had tried and failed a test for fortitude and valor.

She took her time undressing; she moved with studied care as if keeping some violent emotion in abeyance. *Rub its face in it*, she repeated silently, *then toss it outside. Rules are rules.*

She turned on the bathtub's hot and cold taps while her mind began pounding out a dozen questions. She wondered if her attraction to Jim had been pre-ordained, if she'd never be able to reach past her family's turbulent history, if an Illinois farmwife was all she was destined to be. And a fearful, battered one at that.

"Water seeks its own level," she spat out. "Struggle and strive; you only end up in a muddle." The rigid sayings of her aunts and her aunts' austere neighbors clattered into her unwilling ears. "Peas in a pod," she recited, and, "All roads lead home ... A chain is as weak as its weakest link."

She pictured the god-fearing, opinionated faces dispensing aphorisms as readily as horse liniment. "If you sink, you'll never swim ... Be careful what you wish." Then she considered that chimerical creature called Choice. She pictured it standing whole and alone, the embodiment of freedom like a statue in a public park. Choice dominated one pedestal; Dignity graced another; Grief shrouded her head with a marble veil while Truth's superior fist clasped her own stony breast.

She squinted her eyes, trying to avoid the images she'd conjured. *I can make my own way. I don't have to follow Jimmy's wishes, or my aunties', or Poppa's, either—or the Astons', for that matter. I can stay here, or I can leave.* She bent her limber neck in a gesture that had become familiar.

The motion was deceptively slow; to the uninitiated observer the girl would have appeared doe-like and gentle, a young lady acknowledging some minor deficiency. In fact, she was in hiding. The metamorphosis she was struggling to achieve had eluded her once again.

The bath water swirled in the tub, the palest brown from a tinting of rust, and earth-scented as if the hot liquid had only recently risen to the surface of the well. She drew her hand across the bubbling waves.

I got good grades back at home because I worked, she reminded herself. *Because I refused to be like the other kids.*

She stepped into the bath, balancing one foot on the chenille mat while the other plunged down into the mineral-smelling water. *I don't have to care about Jimmy Flaherty. There are plenty of other boys out there. Marriage isn't for me. Not yet. And when it is, I'll find someone different. Someone with my own tastes and education.*

And background? Did you forget where you came from? a persistent voice in her brain began wheedling. *What chance do you have of making a match with a Yale or Harvard boy? The day you're mistaken for a debutante will be the day that pigs sprout wings.*

She sank into the water. She let it rush up to her chest and then her chin, a tidal wave in a porcelain tub. She tipped her head back until the swell engulfed her ears and forehead. She wished she could drown.

***

At that moment, Henry Alston knew he hated his wife. She'd ruined the first chance he'd had to act as Mabel's salvation and comfort. Ruth White had come barging into the kitchen with her foolish prattle about Clarissa's "personal tragedy," and Mabel had fled backwards into the recesses of her cloistered thoughts. Henry doubted he could ever lure the girl out again.

And it was all within easy reach, his furious thoughts argued. *She was mine for the taking. Mine, because she needed me.* Perched on his bed, clad in the dressing gown, pajamas and slippers that would eventually carry him to the bathroom, to the comb, facecloth, toothbrush and mouthwash gargle of his nightly ritual, Henry Alston railed at his fate. *I'm a handsome man. I'm not old yet. I'm vigorous and well-read. I don't have to live a meek existence. I refuse to die before I'm dead.*

"What's that, dear?" Ruth White asked suddenly. Propped on her pillows, with her white hair and pallid cheeks, with her high-necked nightgown and marble-hued fingers, Henry's wife looked like an oracle come miraculously alive. "Didn't my Henums say something?"

"No." The word was leaden and defiant.

She sighed, a long stagy noise that culminated in a martyred moan. "Really, I don't know what to do. I'm at my wits' ends because of that girl."

Although every part of Henry's brain called for a resolution to his feelings about Mabel, nothing would permit a confrontation with his wife. In all their years together, during each little up and down of two distinct beings melding into one single substance, he'd never raised the slightest protest or voiced the merest question. He hunched on his bed, afraid to move. "I didn't say anything. In fact, I didn't speak at all." A hint of desperation colored his performance.

"Oh, my dear! Don't you think I know you well enough to read your thoughts? My Henums can't keep secrets! It's that foolish girl's fault. I've told her so. I've told her so repeatedly. Ever since the beginning, and you know how many moons ago that was!"

Henry's lungs felt as if they'd collapsed into his spleen. His tongue dried up and his eyes forgot to focus. Panic made his wife's words unintelligible.

"Time and again, I've said, 'You upset Henry with your wild notions. You must learn self-restraint. Husbands don't grow on trees. And if mine is any indication, Clarissa, your odd behavior ...'"

Clarissa! Henry finally understood the subject of his wife's speech. *Clarissa!* He coughed the name with the gasp of a man saved from suffocation.

"Clar ... issa!" Ruth White heard sputter in her direction, and then answered with a serene, "Of course, dear! Whoever did you think I meant but my oldest and closest friend—my constant companion since girlhood?"

"Clarissa," Henry repeated. What began as recrimination grew expansive with forgiveness. "Tanmere!" The sound was as indulgent as any stay of execution.

"Oh, I'm so glad you're not cross with the poor thing," Ruth White whimpered. "She's so terribly alone. And she does dote upon a kind sentiment tossed her way."

"Of course!" All the love in the world wasn't enough to pour into his words. "Of course, she does, my dear!"

Henry, in his gray dressing gown, in his heelless slippers and striped pajamas, positively beamed. Smiles encircled him like hummingbirds on hollyhocks. He felt joyous enough to jump up and dance.

"Oh, you're so good, Henums! But then I've always known that. The very bestest husband this little girl can have."

He hadn't heard his wife revert to this childish chatter in a very long time. In fact, he couldn't remember the last time she'd succumbed to baby gibberish. It had been years, he thought, or decades. The flirtatious overture disturbed him. He wasn't certain of the expected response.

Should he walk over to Ruth White's bed and give her dry cheek a little peck? Should he suggest slipping inside her pressed and lavender-scented sheets? Was that what his wife expected?

"I'm glad you're pleased, my dear." He remained on his distant bed, but his voice turned throaty with shammed passion.

It occurred to him that he'd become all-powerful, that his obsession with Mabel could warm the words spoken to his wife or Clarissa, or to anyone. *I can have my cake and eat it too*, he told himself. In order to put his newfound abilities to the test, he stood and walked slowly toward his wife's bed. He let the weight of his body carry his hips forward in imitation of the gunfighters he'd seen in films. "Oooh," he imagined the saloon ladies shrieking; and sure enough, Ruth White produced a similar noise.

"Oooh, Henry," she whispered, sliding beneath the sheets till the coverlet demurely hid her neck. "Whatever can the world's bestest husband be thinking? A work night, too, and a guest in the house."

Suddenly the pretense had gone too far. He stared down at his wife's shriveled body, entombed in bedding so starchy it looked as if no living creature resided there, and he experienced a revulsion so pungent he was afraid he might suddenly vomit. "Just off to the loo. I assume it's finally unoccupied. I'll try not to wake you when I return."

***

Henry struggled down the hall in the wake of Mabel's bath
hour. The walls were awash in the scent of soap and talcum
powder, and the air was thick with girlish fragrances. The
virginal odor of Turkish toweling hung overhead, and something pure and bitter like sun-dried flannelette.

Duplicity is more difficult than I thought, he realized. *A
double life is a tricky business. I'll have to play my cards
right if I'm to succeed.*

His pace quickened as he approached the bathroom door.
In a wild burst of invention, he pictured catching Mabel in
her bath, her naked body slippery and rose-tinged and helpless. She'd try to cover herself, of course, draping a facecloth
futilely across her breasts, but exposing the rest.

Henry's slippers fairly flew.

The door was slightly ajar; light and steam and moisture
as thick as apricot nectar poured into the darkened hall. He
saw beads of water dancing about, like mist invading an
autumnal beach.

The light beckoned. He imagined the empty beach: himself
and Mabel clad only in the sun's warming rays. Mabel's
body would turn luminous, and her face would glow.

He threw open the door.

No one sheltered within the bath's embrace; no one stood
at the window, raising the sash; no one hesitated near the
sink, tooth glass in one hand and facecloth in the other. The
toilet was deserted, and the scales, the linen cupboard and
the hot air vent. It took him only a moment to ascertain his
aloneness, but it seemed to him that he stared into space
for an hour.

"Mabel," he breathed or whispered. He didn't remember
any time during his sixty-odd years feeling so forsaken.

"Mabel," he repeated, and for the first time began noticing the oddness of the place.

First off, there was the matter of the light; Mabel never left the lamp burning when she quit the bathroom. Next, was the tub mat, still carelessly draping the linoleum floor, and her towel that, instead of hanging in regimental folds, had been bunched in a knot on the hook at the back of the door. He wondered if she'd become ill, but the question didn't arouse pity or dread. Another sensation overtook him; he found himself irked at this sudden shift in the rules. It was as if she'd begun a game in which he had no part.

He lifted the tub mat and folded it over the bath's outer lip. The mat still bore the imprint of Mabel's wet foot. The outline was clear, and the arch of her instep and her determined, youthful toes, but his interest was oddly clinical. He reached for the towel. "Ruth White would have a fit if she saw this." He seemed to have become another person.

But not quite. For the last thing to catch his eye was Mabel's cotton panties, balled up in a heap near the bath's claw foot. He stooped down to see them better. It was the first time he'd been so close to his darling's undergarments. As he gaped at the deserted white cotton, every speck of anger left him. He pictured carrying the forgotten piece of clothing to Mabel's door, murmuring through the keyhole and then placing his gift in her embarrassed hands.

He reached down to retrieve the panties. He expected dampness from the steamy air, a scent of innocent perspiration and the remnants of laundry soap. What he didn't expect was a woman's odor and the chalky, frozen residue of love. He dropped the garment as though it had tried to bite his hand.

THE SHOP ON THE HIGH STREET

It was Ruth White's intention to hold a celebratory luncheon in Clarissa's honor, and she divulged this scheme to Henry the very next morning.

"We'll call it a celebration," she said almost as soon as she'd opened her eyes. "Although, of course, there's nothing to commemorate. I doubt there ever will be."

When least expected, Ruth White could be surprisingly blunt. This was true of her dealings with Clarissa, especially. Perhaps the reason was their shared history; adults who've been friends since the age of five often revert to more plain-spoken years when conversing with one another. Or perhaps the cause was merely Clarissa and Ruth White themselves, and the power the one had always held over the other.

"Although it would be nice if she believed we were engaging in some kind of festivity, don't you think? After all, when you come right down to it, we're practically the only solace the poor thing has in this world. Well, that and some musty books. But I'd certainly take a husband any day." Serene in her wifely charms, Ruth White managed a coy giggle from her pillowed bower. She hadn't forgotten the unusual occurrences of the night before, and neither had Henry. Although, at the moment, both were remembering very different events.

"You haven't said a word all morning, Henry!" she twittered. The sound was riddled with suggestive undertones. Henry Alston's wife was growing younger and more seductive by the moment. "And you overslept, as well! Why, you haven't done that in years! If I didn't know better, I'd wonder what the world's bestest husband was up to!"

Henry closed his eyes. He wished he could drive his wife's voice out of his ears. He wished he could go back to sleep and never wake up. He wished daylight would vanish, and night consume the earth.

Who is it? his brain and his heart demanded. *Who's done this to Mabel, and why did she let it happen?* If he could have repeated the previous night's journey to the bathroom, and the subsequent discovery of Mabel's infidelity all over again, he would have done so in a flash—only this time his beloved would have been innocent.

"And so, I thought perhaps that quaint old hotel in Windsor Haven. You know the one I mean. I heard it got quite seedy for a while ... but they say it's been completely refurbished, and the place has that attractive dining room. You remember it, the one with the pretty murals, covered bridges and whatnot. They should appeal to Clarissa's love of history."

Henry groaned aloud.

"Isn't my Henums feeling well this morning?" Ruth White's worried feet pitter-patted to her husband's bed.

"Of course, he isn't! My Henums isn't feeling at all happy. That's why he didn't get up before the cock crowed. That's why he's all huddled in his sheets. The world's bestest husband needs his own, little nurse." She reached a hand toward her husband's brow, but he flinched.

"I'm all right. I just didn't sleep well. Must have been something I ate."

Henry wished his wife would leave his bedside and go about her business. He didn't want her watching him clamber out of the bedclothes. He didn't want her judgmental eyes on his legs or his arms or any other portion of his body.

Why did Mabel do this to me? his brain demanded ferociously, and then equally fiercely pummeled out a promise of retribution: *If I ever catch the scoundrel that ruined her, I'll give him a trouncing he'll never forget! And no one will be able to stop me! I'll beat that boy into sawdust.*

"I'm fine," he snarled, although the words were intended as solace for himself and not his wife.

Rebuffed, though not dissuaded, Ruth White continued to hover near her husband's bed. "I'll just toddle along and do my washing up first, shall I? And then I'll wake Mabel, and you can take your turn in the loo after us two girls. That should give you a little extra time to shake off those mean, old cobwebs."

Before leaving Henry's sheeted figure, Ruth White gave his covered toes a playful squeeze while he, in his hotheaded misery, let out another strangled moan.

***

An invitation note was written and delivered into Henry Alston's hands just as he started to back the Studebaker from the drive. In language flowery enough to summon a guest to Buckingham Palace, the note requested "the honor of Clarissa Tanmere's presence at a festive and commemoratory luncheon."

"Take it directly to the Post Office," Ruth White ordered. "Don't entrust it to the box on the High Street. I've heard those town boys sometimes put nasty things in the letter boxes, and I want Clarissa's invitation to look as though it were intended for a queen."

Or as if it came from one, Henry thought, but he did what he was told. Then he guided the tires over the dirt and gravel of the drive, backed into the lane and headed down toward the High Street.

There'd been no sign of Mabel that morning. By the time he rose, she seemed to have vanished from the house. There'd been no milky glass lying in the sink, no crumb-covered plate near the automatic toaster, no pile of books waiting on the breakfast table, no schoolbag and no yellow sweater.

He hadn't mentioned her absence to his wife. He wasn't quite sure why. It wasn't fear, that much was certain. Ruth White seemed to exist in a world populated solely by her own inventions. He doubted she'd suspect Mabel of wantonness even if the girl took to inviting strange gentlemen into her bedroom.

***

Clarissa fairly blew into Henry's shop. She was breathless as always, but he didn't remember seeing her any other way. He looked up from his stool near the cash drawer, and smiled vaguely as he did with all customers who created more effort than reward.

Clarissa, and a dozen ladies like her, inconvenienced North Chesterfield's merchants on a steady basis. The town's butcher and greengrocer had smiles similar to Henry's, as did the bank teller, the recording clerk, and the postmaster.

He rose and replaced the stool behind the shop's long glass-fronted display case, and was about to offer a noncommittal "Good morning," but Clarissa's words overwhelmed his.

"Oh, Henry! Oh, it's so lovely. And just imagine ... I mean, just think ... Such a lovely spot. Oh, however did you decide on it? Ruth White, I should add. However, did you and Ruth White decide? Because I'm certain you must have instigated the ... Oh, but I couldn't be more thrilled. Honestly. I mean ..."

Terror stopped her cold. She bit her lip, and her eyes edged about as if searching the disapproving father of her haunted memory. "I mean, it is so very kind of you ... you both, to have thought up such a ... such a pleasant gesture. Thrilled, I suppose. Thrilled is rather an overly vehement expression ..."

The mauve silk roses on her lopsided hat bobbed in rapid and dumb agreement, sprinkling dust and a smattering of face powder in the air, and giving the owner of the headgear the appearance of being surrounded by a localized fog. "My father always advised against—"

"Nice hat," Henry interrupted. For the life of him, he couldn't imagine why she'd entered the shop, but if there was one thing he didn't need it was a diatribe about the patriarch and tyrant, Alfred Tanmere. Not today, especially. Not with Mabel disappeared to God knows where, and the routine that had sustained and nurtured him shattered into bits.

He moved away from the stool and cash drawer, and began rearranging a small grouping of fountain pens. The pens were on the very end of the display case's counter top, almost as distant from Clarissa and her tumbled words as it was possible to travel, given the shop's cramped size.

"Oh, do you like it? This ... this little nothing of a chapeau?" She leaned against the display case as she spoke. Or rather she draped herself over it, letting her crepe-covered arms drift across the counter top as one leg kicked backward in a motion vaguely reminiscent of a tango dancer's. The pose might have been an amusing one, but the imitation was in deadly earnest.

"I wore it on purpose," she breathed in a voice newly husky and daring. "I thought you'd like it. You've seen it before, of course ... just as, I'm sure, you've seen all my other ... my other ... *accoutrements*. But not in combination with this purple dress! I suppose, in the past, I considered the outfit rather too bold."

Clarissa attempted an arch, come-hither smile, but immediately knew it as a failure. Conversing with men had brought her grief as long as she could remember, and her only other modes of verbal expression were chats with Ruth White, or responses to queries about library books and card catalogues. On her own recognizance, with no dominant voice to hamper her, she was like a boat without a captain, yawing wildly at the slightest hint of wind or tide. Now her eyes betrayed the certainty that she was, in the words of that ogre, the Patriarch Tanmere "not measuring up."

"I decided that your marvelous celebratory invitation might permit an unexpected gesture on my part—celebrations are so few and far between, after all—so I decided to ... to dress up." Here the words ceased, as if the speaker had revealed more than she'd intended. The brief silence was followed by one of her hee-hawing laughs, and then that was snapped off as well.

"Ah, the invitation. You got it, then." Up until that moment, he'd had no idea why Clarissa had hurried into his shop. Now that he realized the purpose of her mission, he was at a loss for further speech.

During the many years of his wife's friendship with Clarissa, Henry's time with her had been strictly chaperoned. It wasn't suspicion that inspired Ruth White's eagle eye (no one could be attracted to poor Clarissa, after all!), it was merely that Henry Alston's wife liked to be the center of everyone's attention.

He looked at Clarissa, and she looked at him, and not even a millisecond's worth of communication passed between them.

"Mail delivery is certainly quick, these days, I'll say that much," he finally flubbed.

"Oh, yes, it is! The postal workers must all be geniuses, I think!"

Now, Clarissa knew better than to expose her emotions. The fear of ridicule and hurt had been drummed into her at an early age. *Hadn't her father warned her about "being tongue-tied and feather-brained?" Or "building castles in the sky," rather than "behaving rationally?" Hadn't he tried to save her from herself?* However, confronted with her idol, the man of every waking and sleeping dream, she couldn't help herself. "Oh, Henry!"

He couldn't imagine what was wrong with his wife's friend. He wondered if she was having a mild form of stroke, or if—and this seemed far worse—she was suffering from some "mental" ailment.

Ruth White was forever mentioning former friends or neighbors who'd "recently gone mental"; he began fitting the pieces of Clarissa's odd appearance and incoherent conversation together until "mental" became a definite supposition.

"Why don't I take you home, Clarissa," Henry offered. "It's gotten fairly warm this afternoon, and an ... an attractive lady like yourself shouldn't be outside without a sunshade. I'll drive you home in my car."

The words were firm; they were also gentle. *Poor thing,* he told himself, *poor, old thing.* Clarissa's unfortunate state seemed particularly worrisome. He had a glimpse of himself as a lunatic bound for the asylum near the edge of town, a gibbering idiot dragged from his house in ropes and gags and fetters. And all on account of Mabel.

"I'll drive you. It will be a pleasant respite for me to get away from the shop." His tone was soothing, but it needn't have been. Clarissa would have followed him anywhere.

***

Henry drove and Clarissa nestled herself into the passenger seat—Mabel's hallowed spot on the wondrous occasions when she'd graced the car with her glowing presence. As if some aura of youth and innocence remained on the plush upholstery, Clarissa became increasingly girlish while the brief ride progressed.

He turned the car up Bank Street and passed the Merchants Commercial Institution.

"Isn't that the most romantic building?" Clarissa sighed. "All that quiet stone. It's like a great king who has been disappointed in his personal affairs, but who realizes that the well-being of his people and his country rest upon his shoulders."

"Mmm." Henry wondered what novels Clarissa had been delving into recently, or if the cause of this sudden eccentricity were the anthologies of poetry Ruth White had suspected all along.

From Bank, he turned left onto Broad Street, maneuvering past the parked cars that lined both sides of the thoroughfare. It was unusual for him to be out and about at that particular hour and he was astonished at the activity on the sidewalks. The Hygienic Restaurant already sported a goodly crowd; Stanton's Haberdashers boasted a potential buyer selecting a Panama hat from the window display, while a well-dressed couple studied the names on the cinema marquee.

"I always thought I'd have made a marvelous thespian," Clarissa murmured as if relinquishing the one love of her life, "but now I'm too old. Ruth White doesn't know, of course," she added after a hesitant moment. "About my acting ambitions, that is. You won't tell her, will you?"

"No." Henry didn't know how to continue. The idea of Clarissa cavorting about on either stage or screen was an idea too ridiculous to pursue.

He worked his way along Broad Street, amazed at the varied forms of life his town could produce. He watched a farmer and his wife climb out of their dirt-flecked truck, and walk with stiff-shouldered and unnatural calm back down the sidewalk toward the Merchants Commercial

Institution; he spotted a tall young man in rolled shirt sleeves and expensive, rumpled trousers who seemed to collar every passerby in sight and then begin peppering them with questions. Henry's glance swept past the earnest face and the pamphlets and the clipboard and the pen. *He could be my rival,* Henry fumed. *That peach-faced, slim-waisted boy could be the one who ruined my Mabel.* He nearly drove the Studebaker up onto the sidewalk.

"Henry!" Clarissa whispered, then added a diminutive but impassioned: "Dear!"

He didn't hear her; his eyes searched the boy's sandy locks and wholesome jaw while his ears strained to discern the questions the young man was demanding of his audience. *An art student? A politician's aide? A religious zealot? Would any of these types appeal to Mabel? Does she believe in "causes"? Does she subscribe to some arcane philosophical tenet? Does she have thoughts I'll never share?* All of a sudden, he realized he didn't know much about their boarder other than she wore a fuzzy, yellow sweater and a nightie gone threadbare with age. The realization caused his right foot to falter on the gas pedal, and his hands to slump together on the wheel.

He slowed the car to a crawl, and continued along Broad Street till it came to the small traffic circle that led upward to Commons Hill Lane and Clarissa's second floor apartment, or down to Valley Ridge Avenue and the railroad station, lumber yard and river. He glared at every face he passed, whether on foot or in an automobile.

"It is such a marvelously complex structure," Clarissa whimpered in a kind of frenzy as he handed her out of the car. "The ginger breading is Victorian, but the mansard roof is obviously an earlier addition; and, as to the shape, well, one can only assume that the original design must have been saltbox."

Henry hadn't the slightest clue what she was babbling about, nor did he care. He took hold of her gloved hand, and held firm as she began hoisting herself from the passenger seat.

Twisted by the combined efforts of legs and backside, her skirt was lifted well above her wrinkly knees while the wide hem of her taffeta slip poked out with spinsterish abandon. Henry looked away.

"I think of buildings as being sculpted by age, creatures refined by the tests of time. This one's larger than she was as a young habitation, but she's also nobler. Why, that mansard wouldn't work on a lesser house—the one at the end of Commons Hill Lane, perhaps ..."

He stood on the grassy patch of lawn separating sidewalk from street and tried to follow Clarissa's speech. A line of elms shaded the block, eliminating a substantial part of the architectural lecture.

"Houses are ... well, houses are like women, I think. The young ones lack substance, the older ones have learned ... have learned ..." *How to love*, she wanted to say, but she couldn't bring herself to utter the words, nor could she allow the next errant thought to escape. That idea was *how to suffer neglect*, and it was closer to the truth.

"I should be getting back to the shop." Henry backed his feet in the direction of the Studebaker. "You can get yourself upstairs, can't you? See yourself in?"

"Lemonade?" came the frightened response. Clarissa's eyes were already beginning to bulge, and her mouth drawing itself into a self-accusatory grimace: "Can't I get you ...? Invite you upstairs for a moment? A hostess always ..." The gloves clasped each other in despair. *Not measuring up,* the fingers seemed to rasp and grapple. "You needn't rush away ..."

Bats in the belfry, Henry told himself. *Houses like women? What's she going on about?* Then: "Mabel," he murmured as he turned the key in the ignition. It was the second time during the space of one day that the name caused him to feel as emotionally precarious as Clarissa.

CLARISSA'S HOME

Alone in her apartment, Clarissa clung to the door. She'd been barely able to walk up the path to the house's front steps, barely able to step inside the cool foyer or close the curtained French doors. And then the agonizing climb to her small second floor flat! Every wooden board had creaked while the stair rail had stuck to her hand like melting putty.

She'd expected the first-floor residents to poke their heads out of their apartments at any moment, and she'd been certain her two second-floor neighbors would do the same. Step by slow step, she'd dragged upstairs. She'd hardly breathed, but it seemed to her that the noise of her existence was excruciatingly loud. Her taffeta slip had made a sound like sheet metal shaking, and her rundown heels had knocked first against the newel post and then thumped and bumped over each slat of the cherrywood stairs.

Then she'd had to retrieve her key from her purse! And after that she'd been forced to fit the squirming thing into the lock. The key had never seemed so riddled with enmity. It had slithered out of her grasp, leapt to the floor, scuttled under a potted plant and then lodged itself in the dust-ridden darkness where the landlady's cat liked to lick its sneaky paws.

Gray fur had attached itself to Clarissa's fingers, along with the recalcitrant key, and she'd lunged backward in dismay. There'd been no telling if the dark stuff belonged to a feline or a rodent; and the sight of her now-ungloved fingers speckled with fuzz had finally caused her to break down and cry. Right there in the hall! Right there where any spiteful soul could have seen her!

"I've got to control myself," she'd whispered none too quietly. "I'm not measuring up."

Then she'd swung open the door with a noisy bash, and thrust herself into the shuttered shelter of her simple home, clinging to the door handle as if the Headless Horseman, himself, were in deadly pursuit.

"Go away," she'd muttered to the door's varnished boards, although the warning was intended for her own traitorous thoughts. "Go away!" Then, again, came a cruel: *Not measuring up.*

It was fortunate that only Clarissa had the day at liberty. The rumor that "Miss Tanmere talks to herself" had already made the rounds of the building's six other tenants, and been confirmed by six different stories.

"Please go away," she wheedled as she finally turned toward the safety of her sitting room. "Please. Please?" She put both hands to her forehead as if in self-defense, and forced herself to stand erect. "I'm fine. I am."

***

Clarissa's apartment consisted of a sitting room, bedroom and bath. The bathroom had been converted into a bath and kitchenette, and it contained an electric hot plate perched on top of a small icebox and a few pieces of bone china salvaged from the sale of her father's much grander home.

The china was lodged in a corner cupboard that had once been a mere knickknack in the Tanmere household, but like all other mementos of those long-gone times (and Clarissa's three rooms were crammed with them) the cupboard was polished and cosseted and fussed over. Alfred Tanmere's daughter was the keeper of the flame.

"They're all I have left," she'd say, shaking out the antimacassars or dusting the roll-top desk. "They're all I have in the world."

This statement wasn't quite correct, because the apartment also housed a living and radiant being that was Clarissa's secret love.

Birdie was this creature's name, a bright-hued and brighter-voiced yellow budgerigar. Birdie lived in a large and airy metal cage when its owner was away from home (the landlady's cat managed feats of ever-escalating cunning), but when Clarissa returned Birdie was given his freedom.

The overcrowded rooms were the bird's delight. He'd wing himself over to the antimacassar adorning a plush-covered armchair, and then test the silk tassels of a standing lamp while the green baize sofa with its veneered armrests and curving, Victorian back became a jungle garden worthy of Rima, the bird girl. Clarissa would drop whatever minor task she was performing just to stand and watch. Henry Alston and Birdie: those were her two idols, but one was more affectionate than the other.

"Birdie," she now called, returning to the door and locking it fretfully behind her. She scanned the floor as she twisted the key; the landlady's vile cat seemed capable of setting an ambush in any corner of the house. Clarissa believed the heinous creature could shrink in size, slip through a crack no bigger than a peanut shell or pry loose floorboards or scrabble vertically up the building's ancient shingled walls—a cat in league with the devil.

"Birdie! I'm home!"

It took her a moment to accustom her eyes to the darkness of her apartment. She'd never been an admirer of sunlight; it faded her father's precious possessions, and the bright rays seemed overly cheery: good time girls lacking the substance that comes from vicissitude.

"Birdie?" Her eyes began slowly adjusting, but the red, swollen lids were no help. The room remained blurry, as if filtered through buckets of unshed tears. "Birdie? Don't I hear my little Birdie calling his Mama?"

Her stubby shoes shuffled toward the hazy, white object that was Birdie's cage. It stood on a nest of black and red lacquered tables, a group imported by some seafaring great-great uncle back in the clipper ship days. The tables were Oriental, but whether Chinese or Japanese, she didn't know. And of course, with her father dead and gone and his repository of knowledge taken with him, there was no family member left to answer the question.

"Birdie?" By now she was becoming a trifle worried, and she started envisioning large gray clumps of fur padding forward with stealthy self-confidence. In her fear and haste, she crashed into the corner of a gate-leg table.

"Oh," she moaned, without realizing the sound had escaped. "Oh, my knee!" Her leg buckled, dropping her gangly weight onto one of the twin velvet ottomans. She began to weep, and the sound mounted in intensity and loneliness that was out of all proportion to the size of the accident.

"Oh, Henry! Oh, your lovely invitation! And I made such a botch of it! I wanted to ... I wanted to ..." But she wasn't certain what she'd wanted when she'd marched herself downtown to Henry Alston's shop. She had a vague recollection of sipping her morning's cup of Earl Grey tea when the mail had arrived, of opening Ruth White's letter with shaky fingers, of momentarily being unable to decipher the words because of a looming sense of fear. She remembered imagining that Ruth White had finally guessed her secret, that the note must be some kind of threat, or that—and this was a hope that had fluttered straight down from the sky—Ruth White was bowing out and leaving the field (and Henry) to Clarissa.

"Oh, Henry!" she cried, although by now the tears were beginning to subside. "I did my best. I put on all my finery, my newest hose, and ... and ..."A picture of herself, driven ignominiously home in Henry's car, cut off the rest of the words. She saw her purple-clad body lumbering out of the passenger seat; she saw her hat askew and her face aflame, face powder caked on her upper lip and eyelids gone crimson with mortification.

"Henry ..." The name lingered in the air, followed by a louder: "Birdie?"

"Birdie?" She stood, nursed her knee with an absent-minded gesture, then limped toward the nest of lacquered tables and the cage. "Did my Birdie miss me?"

Birdie didn't raise a peep, and Clarissa peered, nearsightedly and still bleary-eyed, toward his favorite perch in the large, white cage. The parakeet couldn't be seen.

She hurried forward. By now, fear had driven all thoughts of the Alston household from her brain. She didn't speak or

whine. Her smudged lips were set in a line that was half
terror and half ruthless determination. The cat that dared
cross her would be sorry indeed. "Birdie!" She reached for
the cage's wire door.

Huddled in the bottom corner, quivering with the slightest
of shudders, crouched a seemingly shrunken Birdie. She
stretched her large, clumsy paw toward him, and the terrified little bird scuttled out of her reach, shook itself all over
and then began panting wildly. Its wings were drawn in
tight, and its head and neck receded in anguish; even the
giddy color seemed muted and dull.

"That damn cat!" Clarissa exploded. "He's been in here
again, hasn't he? He's been pestering my poor Birdie, hasn't
he? Creeping around and licking his chops."

Birdie couldn't answer, of course, but his black eyes stared
up into Clarissa's paler and less expressive ones until she
thought her heart would break.

"My poor baby." She reached both hands toward the
frightened Birdie with a deftness that was surprising.

The parakeet nestled into the coaxing fingers. She could
feel the tiny heart beating and the small lungs gasping the
air of salvation. She pulled the fragile body from the cage
and sheltered it against her purple breast.

"I'll murder that vile cat if I ever catch it in here," she
murmured as she stroked the golden feathers. "I will! I'll
wring its foul neck or stab out its eyes. Or I'll use poison! Soak
a piece of meat in mercuric chloride or ... or laudanum ..."

Then, without intention or even understanding, she began
to cry again. Surrounded by furniture and the dim, gray air
of shuttered windows, she rocked back and forth, cradling
Birdie and closing her eyes to everything that had tortured
her past, and all that might threaten the future.

JIM AND MABEL

Dressed in a nylon slip and nothing more, Mabel sat beside an open bedroom window in the Windsor Haven Hotel. A pair of sepia-patterned curtains shielded her from the road below and the passersby strolling Main Street, but it was the slip, sticking to her clammy skin, that gave her the strongest impulse. She experienced a sense of peril as compelling as any she'd known. It was like climbing the catwalk on a railroad bridge.

The cushioned chair was covered with a prickly, maroon fabric that poked through the slip's thin nylon; she could feel the coarse, scratchy stuff as if she were sitting bare-bottomed in a field of drying hay. She turned slightly, willfully allowing the chair seat to stab at her skin, and then she planted her feet in front of her and stared at her naked toes.

There was a sound from the street—perhaps a car horn, a siren, or even the firehouse whistle sounding noon. She heard the noise but didn't register its meaning. The noise was one more thing she didn't want to consider.

She looked across the room to the double bed, sagging in the middle from too much wear and tear, and at the pine headboard that was randomly spotted as if both giants and dwarves had rested gummy tresses there. Below the headboard were two bunched up pillows, and on one lay Jim Flaherty, face down and motionless like a body drowned in a stagnant pond.

In spite of herself, she had a sudden impulse to run over to him. She pictured his delight as she crawled on top of the bed, tickling his ribs and teasing his sleepy arms. She imagined him turning onto his back and taking hold of her waist while her slip straps dropped from her shoulders.

"You're all mine," he'd say. "All mine. I can't believe it."

Mabel shut her eyes. She didn't open them until she'd moved her head. It was a game she'd played as a little girl. The trick was to picture the place you wanted to go, and not open your eyes till you got there.

Once, when she was five, she'd walked all the way through her aunts' kitchen blind-sighted; she'd maneuvered past the icebox and china cupboard, around the chair where her oldest and fattest auntie shelled peas, and past the step-stool that her thinner but shorter auntie used for reaching the canned goods shelf.

Both ladies had been in the room at the time, as well as Miss Beanno from the Post Office, but no one had guessed Mabel's secret. No one had looked down long enough to see the child's tightly-closed eyes.

It was the zinc-topped table that finally did her in. She'd run her nose directly into its cold, metallic corner as if taking aim, and the blow had knocked her flat. And knocked a good many shrieks out of both aunties, and Miss Beanno, too.

That had been the end of the game. Or the end of it as far as the adults were concerned. What Mabel did in private no one knew. And what she did as she grew older, the aunts and their neighbors had even less of a clue. That didn't prevent gossip, though.

"A secretive child," some suggested darkly. "But so imaginative," others added with hope. "Always inventing a new pastime. It's wise to nourish the life of the spirit. She'll travel far, you mark my words."

And Mabel did keep secrets, although they'd never involved imaginary friends or dreaming she could fly, or even turn into a toad. Her private thoughts had never belonged to childhood.

"I suppose I did go far," she now said. "Compared to everyone else. I left home, for starters. And then I came here." But that final statement unleashed a welter of jumbled memories, and she heard her aunts saying plain as day, "Family is family, dear. We always forgive."

"No," she muttered. "No, we don't." Then her expression turned blank, and her body became as inert as a dress-shop mannequin. It required an effort for her to turn her head. When she did, she stared into the street below the window. A dark blue car and a pea-green car were parked in front of the hotel, their rear bumpers sticking cater-corner out into the oncoming traffic. From her perspective their demise looked imminent, but she knew this wasn't the case. The danger was an illusion.

She didn't know who owned the two cars, but neither one belonged to Jim. His tired, old beast was tucked away on a side street in hopeful obscurity, although Windsor Haven was a good deal removed from the gossiping eyes of North Chesterfield. An entire mountainside lay between the two towns.

After the cars, she studied the trees planted on both sides of Main Street; elms, she guessed, though in her uneducated eyes they could as easily have been maples. They should be, she told herself, with all the syrup and maple sugar the state's awash in.

The elms or the maples were dusty with the passage of many cars; the leaves looked like dyed shoe leather and not something alive, and she suddenly felt extraordinarily sorry for each tree, eking out its mundane existence, dreaming of rain or a respite from the heat, praying that an ice storm would leave its branches intact—hoping for all sorts of things it was powerless to obtain.

Then: *Mount Tom*, she remembered all at once, *Mount Tom and the plane that had crashed on a foggy night. Crashed with a cabin full of passengers. Boys coming home after World War II. Boys no older than Jimmy Flaherty.* For some reason, tragedy seemed everywhere she looked, as if it stalked her on purpose.

"What are you doing all alone over there?" Jim's voice stirred from the bed, startling her so that she shut her eyes with a crunch and then flung them wide open again.

"Thinking." This was partly true, although she doubted worrying over long dead ghosts would be considered practical thought. Not by academic standards.

"I don't want my girl thinking." His speech was muffled by pillows and drowsiness. It sounded as soothing as falling asleep.

She crossed her legs; the movement was less an effort at allure than at self-discipline. *You're in Windsor Haven*, she told herself. *You're fine.* She wasn't certain what lay at the back of her mind, but something was there, prickling and poking as determinedly as the seat cushion.

"What's my girl thinking about?" He pulled himself up to lean on one elbow, smiling at her from the corners of his eyes. The sheet fell away as he moved, revealing his naked body: young and lean and hard, a worker's body not a worrier's.

"Mount Tom ... I don't know why ... Boys your age, maybe ..."

"I don't consider myself a boy, Missy." He chuckled. There was obvious pride in the voice, a man pleased with himself and his world. He stretched across the bed. He was as comfortable on display as any cat. "Though perhaps you've had more experience. Maybe you're an expert on men." He lunged across the bed and made a grab at her slip.

"What makes you say that?"

Jim mistook the anxiety in her voice for flirtation. "That's for me to know and you to find out."

The words shot through her brain. Her face and lips quivered, but she pasted on a smile. Then she willed the past to retreat. The pathetic, dust-choked trees disappeared first, followed by the two cars and their precarious placement. Even the villainous mountainside vanished. *We forgive* began to fade, too, as did her aunts. Her smile grew; it wasn't wholly or even partially genuine but Jim was convinced.

He made a second grab for her slip. "Come on back here."

She dodged out of his grasp. "I wouldn't go calling the kettle black if I were you. I've seen how some of those girls in town look when you walk past."

"Have you?" He grinned.

"Yes, I have." Almost returned to comfortable terrain, she joined in the routine, standing at the foot of the bed—still out of reach but just barely. "I don't imagine you were twiddling your thumbs all those years, just waiting for someone named Missy Gorne to show up."

She moved closer; she kept her eyes on his face, and her lips curved in a coy smile. She seemed wiser and more experienced than her years, as if seduction was a role she'd often played, but the expression was no different than the falsely confident one her aunts and their neighbors had misread so many times before. "That waitress at the Hygienic, for starters. She swanks all over the place when you walk through the door." Expanding on this maneuver, Mabel also became smug. "She'd take you back in a second if she could."

His contented chortle sounded like a lion purring. At least that's how she interpreted the noise.

"Pretty pleased with yourself, aren't you?" She moved one step closer to the bed. "James Flaherty and his conquests."

This last statement unexpectedly crumpled her face.

"Don't, Baby." He took hold of the slip's skirt and began pulling her toward the bed. "Don't think about those other girls."

"I'm not." She didn't say what had upset her, though; she merely took the final step toward the bed. She had her eyes open, but the behavior was no different than the sightless game she'd played as a child.

Tell me about the plane crash, she'd wanted to say, *the boys coming home and the fog rising out of the valley.* She thought those words, but refused to utter them. "Jim Flaherty and his conquests," she repeated in a quieter voice.

"Who's just a danged fool in love." He grinned, pulling her into the crumpled sheets. Her slip wriggled over her head in no time at all, although Mabel was unaware of removing it.

"Let's come here tomorrow," he begged while his hands began to mold themselves to the curve of her back. "I can take another day off, and you can skip classes again."

"I guess ..." Her lips were against his shoulder as she said this; she was concentrating on the salty scent and taste of his skin and obliterating all other thought from her mind.

"You guess!" He pulled away in mock horror. "You guess?"

"Yes. Let's come back tomorrow." Then she wrapped her arms around his shoulders and closed her eyes.

MABEL ALONE

In her own bedroom, returned via the sneakiest of subterfuges: "Late classes! So sorry, Mrs. Alston! I would have 'phoned, but there simply wasn't time ... A surprise examination and everything—as if we were undergraduates again! Oh, I do hope you and Mr. Alston didn't wait for dinner." Mabel considered her new-found life of deceit. The sensation of existing in several different worlds at the same moment was a luxuriant one. *Habit-forming*, she told herself, *the more you do it, the easier lying becomes.*

She flung off her yellow sweater set, and threw both cardigan and pullover onto her desk chair. The haphazard tangle pleased her enormously. "To Hell with it. Who cares for convention? I'm tired of being good and I hate being perfect. I'm going to be like those girls in school—the ones with heaps of money. Maybe I'll learn to smoke, like Jim does, or drink. Maybe I'll take on two lovers at a time. I'll be a temptress without any feelings!"

To prove the point, she produced her own version of a bump and grind. The imitation wasn't very well executed, besides being a copy of a decidedly tame act she'd witnessed in a college revue—a university filled with girls from exclusive homes and exclusive families, a place whose idea of 'bold' was failing to attend Art History Class.

With practice, the dance improved. She pictured herself in a downtown honky-tonk—maybe in Boston or New York, wriggling atop a beer-soaked bar, crushing fingers beneath her stiletto heels while she revealed all or nothing. "To Hell with them!" She swaggered her shoulders and tossed back her hair, put one hand on her hip and struck the most voluptuous pose she could invent.

"Hell and Eternal Damnation! Yes, sir. Oh yes, indeedy!" The words delighted her. They were a slap in the face to her two fierce aunts, and a protest against their sanctimonious, church-riddled friends. "And to the asinine saints in Heaven: you can go to the devil!"

She kicked off her saddle shoes as if continuing the Burlesque routine, and then flipped her white ankle socks into the air. "To Hell with each and every one of you!"

This euphoric condition didn't last long, though. It started to dissipate as she unclasped her strand of glass pearls and was gone before she'd begun to unzip her skirt.

She looked at the darkened bay window. The lilac-hedged view had vanished, reduced to a reflection of a cluttered dresser and herself standing in front of the mirror wearing only her slip and brassiere and pleated skirt. In the night-proscribed stillness of the room, Mabel realized she was utterly alone.

"Hell and Damnation!" she tried softly, but the rebellious sound failed. She stared at the black windowpanes and then at the mirror over her dresser. The bedroom's two lighted lamps splashed a hard brilliance in return, duplicating their image in mirror and windows and obscuring the room's lesser objects with sickly, green-yellow beams.

Mabel raised her arms to the multiple lights. Shadows of her many selves pelted across the ceiling: arms and hands and heads crisscrossing each another like the limbs of marionettes.

"Damn," she repeated quietly, then murmured a nearly silent: "James Flaherty."

She removed her skirt, and laid it on the bed. Then she slid her slip straps from her shoulders. The white nylon quivered as it dropped from her body, then pooled into a heap at her feet. She folded the slip into a small laundry bin.

"That's for the wash. And my panties, too." Her voice was deceptively flat. She unhooked her brassiere and added it to the pile. "Jim ... Jimmy," she whispered, then touched the bone above her heart, pushing against it with gentle insistence as if attempting to recreate a forgotten moment. "That's for strength," she recited his words exactly. "A wish-bone because I wish you'd love me."

Naked, she stared at the dresser mirror. She stood absolutely still, but it seemed to her brain that she might have been running down stairs or doing cartwheels or struggling free of a house on fire. She was anything but calm.

"Jim," she said again, and then shut her eyes tight. *Crying's for cowards,* she told *herself, and babies and people who never learned how to hope. I'm too tough for tears. I'm too* ... But the tears very nearly won.

***

At his peep-hole in the bathroom, Henry watched Mabel's every move. He could see her lips open and close, but couldn't catch the words. Twice he'd been tempted to put his ear to the crack in the wall rather than his eye, but listening would mean missing Mabel's performance.

Because that's what the dance seemed to be. A performance of the most hedonistic sort. *She must be drunk*, he told himself with a combination of fascination and dismay. *That's why she came home so late. That was the reason for all her excuses. She was out drinking with that fellow. Whoever that damned fellow is. That damn fellow who's trying to ruin her life.*

It would never have occurred to him to picture her and a lover in a hotel bedroom. He couldn't have said the words, let alone faced the thought.

"Out drinking," he whispered. "Out painting the town red with other young women and men. Talking about Heaven knows what, and doing even worse, I suppose."

As if on cue, Mabel swept off her sweaters and shimmied her shoulders, then she dropped both garments in a heap on her chair, and curved her lips into a pout of self-satisfaction. When that trick was finished, she lifted her arms to the light, seemed to study herself in the window's reflection then slithered out of her skirt and wiggled her hips.

Henry had never witnessed anything so enticing. Nothing could have wrenched him away from his front row seat. Ruth White might have been expiring at his feet, or his dry goods shop consumed by flame; nothing but a direct appeal by Mabel would have dragged him from the bathroom wall.

"Out carousing with some young swain." The new and daring Mabel was proving more irresistible than her meeker counterpart. At that moment, Henry, at his solitary vigil, and Mabel, careering around her room, had created nearly identical personae.

This composite creature slithered wanton fingers toward a slip strap, then caressed the satin ribbon till it dropped from one shoulder. He opened his ecstatic mouth, but no sound came.

"Yes, sir," she seemed to murmur in his ears alone. "Yes, oh yes, indeedy."

She stared seductively at the dresser mirror as her hand crept toward the second strap. The look was one of pure indulgence. Henry could see this exchange clearly: Her gray-brown eyes and still-swollen mouth beckoning her counterpart as if the mirrored and living women were urging each other toward greater acts of debauchery.

The second slip strap fell, and he almost banged his head on the wall. "Dearest," he muttered, and then, "You little whore."

As if the words were audible, or perhaps because the thought entered her mind at precisely the same moment, Mabel began a sinuous laugh. "Hell and Eternal Damnation," she whispered into the dresser mirror. "Yes indeedy."

The white slip shimmied toward her waist and then cascaded over her hips. She writhed as the nylon fluttered to the floor, then she stubbed the fabric with a toe and smiled and licked her lips.

"Darling," Henry moaned from one side of the wall while Mabel, on the other, grinned, "Yes, sir."

Finally she stood naked and motionless, gazing at the dresser mirror while he waited, anticipating some new and more titillating delight. But she remained immobile, her vamp eyes half-shrouded, while her lips stretched languidly, forming a single, rapturous word.

Henry, he could almost hear her say; and he jammed his body so close to the wall he marveled he didn't burst through.

"Dearest," he whispered while Mabel shut her eyes, then turned in a swooping curve and stared directly at the hole in the plastered wall.

THE HOTEL IN WINDSOR HAVEN

That night Mabel dreamed. It was an activity she didn't indulge in ordinarily, and when she did, she was careful to erase the images as soon as she woke. But her encounter with Jim Flaherty had shifted something within her soul, or perhaps the trigger had been her willful shimmy in front of the mirror.

The dreams were a haphazard shuffle of memory and invention. She saw the same hound dog puppy that had soiled her aunties' favorite rug, and the next moment she was staring at the terrified animal grown. Grown and cowering beside the speckled stone of a barn's rear wall. The creature's ears were flattened to its dome-shaped skull and its tail twisted between its legs to protect a panting, brown-black belly. A man with a horsewhip stood above the whimpering beast, raising the knotted rawhide again and again.

"Stop it," the girl, Mabel, screamed in the dream. "Poppa, please! You'll kill him!"

Escaped to the Alstons' house, she witnessed this brutal murder a second time.

"Please, Poppa, please!" she wailed in unison with her own childhood screams.

Then the adult Mabel stood on a mountain-backed beach, a place her land-locked existence had never visited before. Waves were breaking on the rocky sand, carrying both animate and inanimate detritus onto the salt-racked land. A broken chair washed forward, then the sodden trunk of a tree; a piece of a storm cellar door crashed above the foamy brew and seaweed by the armful. Her dead dog was trapped within the slimy, brown stuff, its skin and hide in tatters as if it had been flayed.

"Poppa, stop! I'll tell, Aunty. I will." She shouted to the air, then whirled around, staring at the shale and scrub-covered cliffs, convinced that some malevolent creature was lurking there. *I'll tell.*

***

Mabel worked hard to eradicate those nightmares. From the moment she opened her eyes, while she dressed, ate her brief breakfast, then climbed aboard the public bus bound for Mt. Simmons College, she told herself that dreams were "dumb" and that people who believed them were "irresponsible."

Sitting through morning class and later walking toward the library, she chastised herself for "inventing devils and phantoms." She had many years of fire-breathing sermons to back her up. Her aunts had been rigorous when it came to religious education. Mabel clenched her eyes against the monster of the dream; she tugged at her strand of glass pearls and tidied the pleats on her skirt; she pictured herself as the carefree young women she emulated, and gradually her wishes won out.

She was able to meet Jim Flaherty near the concealing shelter of the college's wide, stone entrance gate with something resembling a blithe and easy heart. She was determined to outstrip her past.

***

"I don't know, Jimmy. They're so supremely old-fashioned. I mean, they're very sweet and everything, but I just haven't been able to bring myself to tell them yet. They're awfully naive about the world ... and boyfriends and everything ... well, you know what I mean ... I bet they never even have sex!"

Jim, sprawled against one lumpy, hotel pillow and Mabel, now equally naked and happy, laughed until the antiquated mattress shook.

"I don't think they do. Really!" She reached across the tangled sheets and rested her hand on his chest. The movement appeared effortless and relaxed; she might have been doing this for years.

"Anyway, I can't tell them anything right now. Not till after that silly luncheon's over. It's going to be a very big deal. Mrs. Alston's got everything planned. Calling it a 'festival' and keeping the arrangements secret. She's like a little kid. I have no idea why she included me. Wanted to make it more of a party, I guess—"

"It sounds like the three of them make enough of a party, as it is." The interruption was full of innuendo. He caressed her hand as he spoke. Like her gesture, his was equally easy. The difference in their two encounters at the Windsor Haven Hotel was remarkable. "A neat, little threesome."

"Jim!" Mock horror made her laugh again. "You know what I mean!" She turned her face toward him and her hair swung across the pillow. "You have a terrible mind, James Flaherty. Remind me not to engage in any more serious conversations." The word 'engage' took on a peculiar ring; it clanged like water lodged in her ears or a dive through duckweed at the bottom of a murky lake. She hoped he didn't notice.

"It's your fault, Missy. You bring out the worst in me." If he'd heard her falter, he didn't show it.

"Oh, Jimmy! You know that's not true!" A giggle became camouflage for emotions too ambivalent to examine. "Look at all the new things you've taught me! Besides, you'd never say those disgusting things if you knew Ruth White and Clarissa Tanmere! I feel sorry for her. I mean, can you imagine a life like that?"

"Like what?" He rolled toward her and touched her shoulder. It was obvious his thoughts were a long way from Clarissa or Henry or Ruth White.

"Being a spinster and everything? Never having a boyfriend, or being in love ... or ... or doing what we're doing right now?" She wriggled under his touch as his hand slipped to her breast. *This part was fun,* she thought, *and so much simpler than thinking about the future or the past.* "You're awful. And I bet you've never been any different."

There was a good deal of pride in these words; they were a challenge to every other woman he'd bedded. Mabel wanted to believe herself the best, if not the first; but she needed him to tell her so. "I can just imagine the racy things you've said to your other girlfriends. And done ..." Here the effort crept onto shakier ground. She definitely did not want to think about him in bed with anyone but herself. She didn't want to picture him at the hotel in Windsor Haven or anywhere else, for that matter. "That waitress at the Hygienic, for instance ..."

"You two are getting to be regular buddies, aren't you?" The response was oddly business-like. "It seems every time I turn around you're bringing up her name. You ladies can become the future Miss Tanmere and Mrs. Alston."

Mabel didn't open her mouth. The labels of Mrs. and Miss hit too close to home, as well of the fatalistic ties inspired by small town life.

Jim chuckled at her silence. "I can tease you back. It's a two-way street." He reached for her other breast and squeezed.

"Ouch," she muttered, although the pain wasn't physical. There was something disturbing in his voice and behavior, a taunting approach out of step with the peaceful coziness of the afternoon. "Don't do that." She moved out of reach. Her tone was soft, but her face and body had turned stony. Lying on the edge of the bed, she stared at him as if he'd become a person she'd never met.

"You like to get your own way, don't you?" Again, the voice and words were unexpectedly harsh. "Mabel," he tacked on, but this cruelty was unnecessary. She was already biting her lip and pulling the soggy sheet close her chin. "Just like Clarissa Tanmere. All dolled up and nowhere to go."

If she'd been a wiser person, she might have whispered, "Why are you doing this?" or she might have gotten out of the bed and found her clothes and left. If she'd been older and more experienced, she could have looked at the situation and made any number of decisions.

But she was neither old, nor wise. Jim Flaherty wasn't either of those things, either, although she didn't realize it. In her eyes, he was a man of the world, a man who knew his way around. And despite her protestations about education and career, the well-spoken young men who dated the Simmons girls paled in comparison. They were spineless and spoiled, boys who depended on weekly allowances sent from home and not on the rough and tumble existence of earning their daily bread.

"A wizened old maid like Clarissa." Whatever was troubling him wouldn't let go.

Mabel closed her eyes. "Don't."

"So, when do you plan to tell them about us?" Winning, he turned mean, although it wasn't clear who deserved the punishment. His face twisted as if waiting for an attack. "After this famous luncheon party? Or are you just going to walk out their door? Or maybe you never meant those things you said. Maybe I'm only useful while you're here. A rube from some pokey place in Massachusetts, someone who doesn't know any different. Someone you'll leave behind without a second glance." The growing rage in this speech surprised him as much as Mabel.

"Don't," she whimpered while he flung out a fury-filled and self-pitying:

"'My year with the town cop—I remember it well. He was such a simple beast, poor dear!'"

Mabel pictured herself someplace far away, somewhere verdant and lovely, full of apple trees in lacy blossom and a scent of promised honey in the air. There were ferns unrolling fiddle-neck leaves and daisies spreading a white-petaled carpet. And birds, too. Birds skittering over every bough: goldfinches warbling and titmice twittering, and now and again the soothing coo of a nesting dove. In her mind, she wandered all around that wondrous haven.

Her body didn't move, however; it stuck to the sheets as though molded there. While Jim, as distant as a double bed could take him, roiled around, bumping his calves against the mattress and banging his shoulders into the pillow.

"I hate these hotel beds," he spat out. "The springs are shot from too much sex." The description was intended to make her recoil, and it worked. Her body became even more inert and her clenched eyelids ceased fluttering altogether.

"I bet you're thinking I've been here a bunch of times." The words shot ceiling-ward, spattering everything with vitriol and pain. "With Rose from the Hygienic, or any number of people. I bet you've spent all afternoon counting bodies ... and yesterday, too. You'd like me to be some no-account low-life who spends his nights getting girls in trouble."

Mabel didn't answer, but tears began rolling slowly down her cheeks. She was powerless to prevent the display. Instead, she concentrated on her imaginary garden, adding a brook at one end, and watercress growing leafy and bitter in the sun-dappled shade. But the brook unexpectedly turned foul, and its rocks became slimy with bloodworms. Then drought beset the meadow, and the apples trees withered and their leaves turned as sere as the ones wilting in the road below the hotel. "Don't," she whispered through lips that barely opened.

"Then why don't you tell them? Why don't you say 'I've gotten myself engaged to James Flaherty and I'm going to go live with him'? Why do you keep lying all the time? Talking about Clarissa Tanmere and her dopey hats, and all that other stupid stuff? Lunch parties and things I'm never invited to?"

The questions were simple ones, but Mabel didn't have any answers. Every invented response was riddled with indecision.

I don't know, half of her wanted to say while the other half wished it could hide its head. *I think I love you, but then I don't know ... And anyway, I can't marry you. I can't spend my life in North Chesterfield. I have no idea why I said I would.*

His furious voice rode across these silent replies. "Why can't we go to my place instead of coming here? Why do we have to find a hotel, for God's sake? You're not a queen, you know."

Moment by moment, he felt her mind hurrying away, dismissing him as a clod and an oaf, a minor fling, a joke. The harsher this self-criticism, the more he fought back.

"You're not so high and mighty, Mabel."

"I thought your landlady wouldn't approve." This was the first coherent sentence she'd spoken since he'd begun his diatribe; she had no idea what made her choose the words, and she knew as soon as she uttered them that the impression was wrong. I've got to set him straight, she'd told herself over and over, but time and again she'd taken the opposite approach.

"To Hell with my landlady!" he almost yelled. The tone had changed completely; this time the noise bustled with relief. "Besides, when I tell her we're engaged, she'll be all smiles. You wait and see!"

Mabel's closed eyes squinted into tighter slits, but instead of speaking up, she reached a tentative hand across the bed.

With that single gesture, her aunts roared back into view, and then her father stumbled toward her again, reeking of liquor and unwashed clothes. She flinched, but the memory clung to her. It was as though she'd never climbed aboard a bus bound for Massachusetts, never found a sanctuary with the Alstons. Her shoulders sagged in defeat.

Seeing her spine curve, Jim believed his love had finally conquered her fears. "You're great, Missy." Sitting up, he leaned in as he spoke, desperate to make amends. "You are. I'm a dope. I shouldn't yell at you. I'm sorry. I am. I'll never do it again."

"That's okay," She rolled on her side and forced her eyes open.

"You're great, Mis," he repeated and then slid his body so close to hers that not even air came between them.

***

Mabel awoke with a start. The room was pitch black, although she could make out headlights from a single passing car. Their reflection jiggled across the wall, caroming around as if the car's tires were bouncing across a field full of stones. For the life of her, she couldn't remember where she was.

She'd been dreaming again. That much was certain. A fire at home, and the old barn consumed by flame. The horse had been rescued, and the cow and then some of the chickens, but the building burst apart at the seams. Sparks as loud as gunfire exploded upward through the night sky, and a heat so intense it seemed to sere the skin.

"It must have been all that hay your Poppa stored there," she'd heard a neighbor's voice shout above the din. "Hay's no better than tinder if you keep it too long. I told him.

I did. But the man wouldn't listen. And gasoline, too ... I must have warned him a hundred times, at least—"

"Hurry! Quick!" another man had yelled. "Come on before the house goes up as well. Those two women are still inside."

"Your Poppa's in the house with them, ain't he? He's not on one of them benders in the barn, is he? Or in that old shack of his? Cause if so ..."

"Oh God, no ..." she echoed, yelling and jerking upward in the hotel bed.

Another car drove past in the road below, and this time the lights careened over a different wall. The bed's headboard turned a glaring white before the shadows shot down to Jim's sleeping face. For a moment, she didn't recognize him, so engulfed was she in the semi destruction of her former home. Before she could prevent it, her mind's eye witnessed the barn's collapse. Neighbors raced toward the house.

"Oh, my God!" she screamed.

Jim awoke. "Mabel? You okay?"

What could she say without dredging up a history she'd been trying to outrun?

"We're late. That's all. I've got to get back. Oh, God. What am I going to tell the Alstons?"

"That it's no good closing the barn door after the horse has escaped?"

He chortled, but Mabel began to moan.

"Hey, there now. No need to carry on. It's only nine o'clock. You've been out this late before."

"It's not that ..."

"Well, what's wrong, then?"

"I don't know. A bad dream."

"Don't want my beautiful girl having nightmares."

But the words "mare" and "barn" only made her huddle further into herself.

***

The return to the Alston household was silent: Jim, feeling confident that he'd finally won his lady's heart, and Mabel too panicked to speak. The night air was warm and fragrant and foggily damp. The scent of honeysuckle wafted in through the open windows and the chirrup of swamp-dwelling frogs advertising for a mate. There were fireflies as well, sprinkling their phosphorescent glow over the open fields and into the deepest woodland. Jim reveled in each physical sensation. Mabel shrank from them, hiding herself in his one-armed embrace.

Things will turn out for the best, she tried to assure herself. *He'll understand when the time comes. At least, I hope he will. No, I'm sure he will. He's a man, after all. He's had other girlfriends. I'll get my degree and move on. It will be difficult, of course, but we'll act like adults. Un' affaire de coeur, that's what I'll say. Un' affaire de coeur. And I'll choose an unorthodox career, or … no, I'll become a lauded poet like Edna St. Vincent Millay, and win prizes and be adored … or … or maybe H.D. and travel to Greece and write about ancient heroes and battles …*

Jim, oblivious, held his girl close and watched the headlights sweep across the macadam road as if he were surveying an exclusive domain.

RUTH WHITE SLEEPS

Lying in wait on his unruffled bed, Henry heard the kitchen screen door swing open. The sound crept up the side of the house and tiptoed through the window sash, a noise terrified of scandal and confrontation.

He kept perfectly still, ignoring Ruth White's snores and his own halting gasps. The door shivered on its hinges with the gentlest of squeaks, and softly closed again. Then he heard two voices whispering together, indulging in soft, merry sounds that seemed to mock the lateness of the hour and the darkness of the staid and tidy house. Henry wanted to turn on his bedside lamp, but something pinned him in place. It felt as though a creature larger and stronger than himself had control of his body. "If she brings him in here," he muttered under his breath, "if she brings him up here ..."

He couldn't finish the threat. He had no idea what terrible deed he'd perform if Mabel and her young swain were to walk up the front hall stairs.

"At least I assume he's young," Henry mumbled. The possibility that his rival might be something other than a callow youth was suddenly terrifying. An older man wooing Mabel! The thought was intolerable.

He rasped out a few jerky gasps, and his hands fumbled confusedly across the sheets. But his ears stayed alert! Oh, his ears kept careful score.

Below the bedroom window, Mabel was laughing with a low and intimate gush that Henry had never heard. Then she leaned against the screen door; and he followed every move as his beloved's body pressed itself into the copper netting. Her sultry slide caused the night-dampened paint of the doorframe to creak, and the dew-soaked hinges to whistle.

She's kissing him! Henry told himself. *Kissing the bastard right under my nose!*

This was the first time in his life he'd used such vulgar language. He'd always been so careful around Ruth White, and before that, too—a line of circumscribed and careful years. Henry began to feel supremely cheated, a man who'd toed the line while others stepped blithely around it. "Bastard!" His chin jabbed skyward and his white hair bristled with electric rage.

"Mmmm?" Ruth White stopped snoring, although she didn't fully waken. Decades of communal, if distant, living had attuned her ears and thoughts to Henry's slightest whim. "Mmmm?" The sound was muzzy with dreams and pillow down.

"Nothing ... Nothing dear." In his mind, he pictured Ruth White awake and alert as a tigress protecting her young. She'd fly down the stairs, prepared to beat back the intruder, the despoiler of Mabel Gorne; and Henry realized he'd be horribly disappointed if she did. Despite every jealous anxiety, he knew he had to let Mabel and her lover continue.

"Nothing at all." The words fluttered soothing noises, the kind pigeons make, or nurses on a terminal ward.

Ruth White resumed her snoring.

A metronome in Henry's brain counted the beat. *Don't come inside yet,* he begged the invisible Mabel, *please don't wake the old bag up.* Here again, the unseemly phrase rattled him, made him lose track of Ruth White's cadenced snores, and shook him to his bones. *What's become of me?* he wondered frantically. *I can't allow myself to behave this way.*

Then "Fuck!" he added in a noise that banged against his ears like popping corn. He'd never used that vile word before. His terrified eyes stared at the ceiling while his body seemed to drop away from the bed entirely. He wondered whether the physical thing that was himself, that housed his muscles and tendons were in the act of turning into someone else, someone unrecognizable and foul: a mod-suited boy with long hair and trousers as slim as pencils, the kind of person who got girls into "trouble."

At that moment, a male voice rose from the kitchen door and passed unconcernedly through the curtained bedroom window. The voice coaxed and wheedled; it was full of its own desires, and heedless of any other.

"No," Henry heard Mabel giggle, and he realized that what he wanted was to watch the two together. Watch them from the hidden crack in the bathroom wall, memorize every movement as their bodies rose and coupled, illumined by the arcing glare of the room's electric light.

"No. I told you the old folks would never understand!"

The old folks, Henry's brain echoed. The vision of Mabel in bed was dashed in a moment. She no longer engaged in lewd behavior for his benefit. She didn't give him a second thought. The lights of the invented love nest turned instantaneously black while Henry pictured himself standing alone by the darkened bathroom wall with his pajamas coiled limply around his feet.

"To Hell with them both!" he said aloud.

Ruth White's snores stopped in a trice. "Henry ...? Is my Henums awake?" Between each word lay an ocean of sleep. Demi-dreams bobbed about and curious visions, but Henry heard the truth. If he didn't take immediate action, Ruth White would awaken.

"Nothing, dear," he intoned in his most soothing manner. "I merely have to visit the toilet. Nature calls, my dear."

The words were familiar enough for unconscious translation. Ruth White was soon snoring again, and Henry kicked free of the sheets and grabbed up his dressing gown.

But what to do next? He realized he couldn't prowl down the hall to the bath. Mabel might swing up the stairs at that self-same moment—with or without her beau. If she saw him in his rumpled, stubbly state, she'd lose all respect; and if her beau stood grinning by, then Henry would be forever damned.

"Fuck!" The word seemed to shatter the air and burst through his soul. "Oh, Fuck! Fuck this shit!"

The whites of his eyes turned as dry as beans; his tongue grew stiff and his throat forgot to swallow. He sidled toward Ruth White's bed; the hairs on the back of his neck bristled and his ears pounded as though blood and sand engorged them.

"Oh, shit!" But by now, the words had lost every ounce of their power. He was a man beyond the pale. "That whoring bitch," he said, and crept into the moonless shadow beside Ruth White's bed.

At that moment, fresh from her amorous goodnights, Mabel tripped along the upper stairs, passing the landing and starting across the hall. The blood in Henry's eardrums receded, and he heard her girlish sighs as she reached her door and flicked on the light.

"Yoohoo... Are you both awake?"

Henry was stunned by her behavior. He imagined her telepathic or able to see through doors; it never occurred to him that she might simply want to talk.

"I am," Henry half hissed. "Mrs. Alston's asleep, though. She's had one of her 'nights.'"

"Oh, that's too bad." Disappointment carved holes in the tone. She didn't ask after Ruth White's health, so Henry wasn't forced to lie again.

"Well, goodnight," she called and shut her door without waiting for a reply.

Alone beside his wife's bed, Henry cursed himself and the world with the vilest phrases he could dredge forth. He felt frazzled beyond belief, and his head was pounding. Everywhere he looked, familiar objects grew sickly and pale. The moon's slim beams imbued the place with a blue-whiteness; the chair at his footboard looked submerged and rotten; even Ruth White's bedstead seemed to grow sea-moss and crustings of barnacles.

Breathing deeply and drawing the air into his lungs as though afraid of suffocating, he reached for the wall. There were no words to express the hatred and disappointment he felt toward himself; and so he didn't use words. He neither berated himself for being a coward, nor railed against the lifelong habit that carried him, slipper-shod, to his bed every night at precisely the same hour. Nor did he find fault with his wife or his job or the safe confines of his house. Instead he ground his teeth together with such force that his jaw seemed in danger of shattering under the pressure. And he whimpered. Without intending to, he mewled several inarticulate cries.

"Does my Henums have a tummy ache?" he heard from somewhere near his knees.

"No." He opened his eyes for the same reason, and saw that the moon's light had shifted, covering Ruth White as well as her pillow and quilt. His wife's hair made a mat around her face that was as dense as snow. The snowflake coiffure seemed the only living thing on the bed.

"No, I'm fine." He sat on the edge of Ruth White's mattress. He had no idea where this strange gesture came from. If his wife had quizzed him, he might have answered: "A sudden cramp in my calf" or "Fatigue, pure and simple," but his sudden invasion of the bed had nothing to do with those excuses.

Ruth White struggled out of her husband's way. "No tummy ache?" Her voice fluted in a high-pitched, tenuous tone. She could feel warmth emanating from Henry's thigh, and with the heat came a smell as pungent as steaming cabbage leaves.

"No." He didn't move.

Ruth White tried to accommodate him, but the narrow bed ran out of space, forcing her to curve her stick-like body around her husband's more solid frame. She waited for him to speak; she waited for him to rise and walk away, but he remained, immobile and pulsing out spasms as hot as a furnace.

"My Henums isn't thinking naughty thoughts, is he?" she ventured with a giggle more fearful than coy. "He's not imagining wicked things, is he?"

"Yes," he moaned, and toppled sideways onto his wife's pristine pillow. Ruth White couldn't have seen it, but his eyes were swelling with tears.

"Help me," he all but sobbed.

Ruth White had long-since forgotten the motions necessary to ensure her husband's relief. Lack of practice and a steadfast prissiness had buried every germ of knowledge; and so she scuttled to the farthest edge of her mattress as if she'd been confronted with a request as terrifying as taking the controls of a runaway locomotive.

"Well, dear. It's so very late, and I haven't been sleeping at all well. Little worries, I daresay. But still, I don't believe I'd ..."

"Help me." He lunged across her body, covering her mouth with a slimy kiss.

"Oh, my dear. My dear!" Ruth White fought out the words. Her husband's tongue pressed between her teeth, and his lips seemed in danger of swallowing hers in a single gulp. "We can't ... I shouldn't ... It's late ..."

"God damn it, Ruth White!" he roared, and she grew instantaneously limp.

The bedclothes flew from the mattress, and the pillow crashed to the floor. "I can't ... I can't ..." he moaned, but it was obvious that whatever his failings were they had nothing to do with Ruth White.

"My dear?" she tried to gasp out again. Repelled and revolted, her mind had closed down, leaving only the simplest of phrases behind. It was as if she were reciting responses someone else had written. "You're bruising my arm." Never mind what Henry Alston was doing to the rest of his wife's body, her attention circled around the one object she could safely discuss.

The noise was enough to disturb him, however. Polite conventions rear their demanding heads when least expected; and his practice of mild-mannered acquiescence caused him to pause long enough to allow Ruth White a momentary escape. She scurried to the other side of the bed. "Oh, my ..." A vestige of coyness clung to the tone, while an imitation smile molded her lips. Nothing on this earth would have permitted the expression of other emotions. She couldn't have drawn up wrath-filled recriminations, or accused her husband of brutality even if every saint in heaven had come down to cheer at her side.

"Oh, my," she repeated with a despairing trill. "I suppose we're never too old ..."

But the word 'old' was one she never should have used. It caused Henry's eyes to burn and his lips and earlobes to feel as though they'd been scalded. "Old! Oh, Jesus!"

"Henry!" Ruth White admonished. Habit was habit, after all; her flannelette nightgown could have been bunched ruthlessly around her waist, her hipbones mangled, and her shoulders twisted in their sockets, but a facade of decency must remain. "I don't know what's come over you." The voice was no longer timorous.

"Jesus, Mary and Joseph! God damn it to Hell!"

If her husband's violent attempt at lovemaking had caused Ruth White to recoil, his oaths were worse. She'd never heard language like it, and never believed her husband had either. She closed her eyes, shut out the moon and the night, the lilac burgeoning and the narcissus waning, the young grass, and the dew-covered baby maple leaves. She obliterated the sounds of the house, as well: the creak on the stairs as the floorboards grew cold, the serene, old tock of the sitting room clock and an elm bough brushing the roof. She refused to hear or smell or listen.

"Old! Old! Oh, Christ!" He grabbed his wife's skinny waist and thrust himself up and over her, pinning her in place. Tears soaked his face, and began sweating over Ruth White's as well. *Mabel*, his heart pounded, *Mabel, my darling, my love.* What he said, though, as he barked and begged toward his crescendo was: "I've got to have you, dearest. I've got to."

THE CELEBRATORY LUNCHEON

The next day was Clarissa's "festival celebration." Ruth White woke later than usual, and Henry did, too; the only early riser of the threesome residing in the house was Mabel. She slipped in and out of the bathroom without making a sound, dressed herself in a pink wool scoop-necked dress (the nicest she owned), attached her hose to her garter belt with four definitive slaps, and fastened the clasp on her glass pearls. Then she crept down the front stairs.

The sensation of finding herself alone in Mrs. Alston's kitchen made Mabel smile. Setting the teakettle steaming, then boiling two eggs and slathering butter and blackberry jam on her toast, she felt as if she were playing house. She even started singing. Jittering around between the stove and dining alcove, she began first humming and then twanging out an odd assortment of tunes.

"'Our Father's God, to thee ...'" she chanted from "America," then followed with a rousing verse from the Old One Hundred Twelfth:

"'The tumult and the shouting dies, the captains and the kings depart; still stands thine ancient sacrifice, an humble and a contrite heart ...'"

But the strangest refrain was an impromptu medley she created from "If I Loved You" and "I Don't Know Why." Half-humming and half-crooning, she never stopped grinning. But then she never began thinking, either.

***

Upstairs, in the Alstons' bedroom, Ruth White was the first to hear the commotion below. She became aware of it before opening her eyes, and for a moment she feared the noise might have been created by Henry—Henry on another unfathomable rampage.

But Ruth White was not a lady to run home crying. Besides, she reminded herself, she was already home, the place she and her illustrious relatives had built from the hardscrabble soil of New England. She took a deep, rejuvenating breath, straightened her spine and stretched her toes toward the footboard in rigid and parallel lines. Then she flung her eyelids open.

The morning was already thick gold and bright. High-tossed clouds and the chirps of many determined birds circled the air with dizzying speed, while the dotted-Swiss curtains blew inward from the window sash in billowing gusts. "Get up!" each image and sound seemed to order: "Get up! Get up, you lazy bones!"

"Oh, my," she said in unconscious repetition of her previous night's words. She looked across the room to Henry's bed and was relieved to find him properly in place, and also to see that he was still asleep. She twisted her hips below the bedclothes. They felt bruised and tired, as if she'd been climbing a steep hill, but the sensation carried with it a new-found youthfulness and elasticity. "Oh, my." From her

124

tone, it was clear that her ordeal had passed into another terrain. Whether this change was due to Massachusetts stoicism or to some more personal revelation, even she couldn't have said. "Well, well. Life is certainly filled with surprises." For once, she was at a loss for an instructive homily from her mother or grandmamma.

Henry woke at that moment. He lay curved on his side, both arms between his drawn-up knees and his chin buried deep in the pillow. He heard his wife's words, but didn't move. If he could have traded places with any human being on the planet, he would have done so without a moment's hesitation. He would have transformed himself into a hooked rug, if necessary, or a standing brass lamp—anything to escape the tears and vilification he was certain were about to be leveled at his head.

"Mabel," he whispered under his breath, but the magic invocation failed.

"Goodness! Look at the time," he heard. "And today of all the inappropriate beginnings. Clarissa's promised fete! Rise and shine, Henry. We mustn't be late. And listen to those birdies chirping. Why, the world's alive and dancing!"

These words were so unexpected that he could do nothing but obey. He clambered from beneath the covers, reached for his dressing gown and then slid one arm after the other into his dark gray sleeves. He kept his back to his wife all the while.

Confronted with her husband's hulking figure, Ruth White turned inexplicably shy. Watching him, she huddled deeper into her bed and her chatty speech dried in her throat. "You use the loo first. Mabel's obviously stirring already. And I'll ... well, of course, I can always wait." A fluttering laugh didn't mask her discomfort.

"Your pajama bottoms are all awry, my dear," she added in voice so quiet it sounded as if she were facing certain death.

Henry didn't answer.

***

The kitchen buzzed with activity. Henry, dressed with the greatest of care in his nattiest suit, and Ruth White, accoutered from head to toe in robin's egg blue, bustled about the room while Mabel, still clad in unsullied pink, bumped in and out of their way as she tidied her own breakfast dishes and carefully refolded the newspaper before returning it to the stool beside the outside door.

The sight of the door gave her a momentary pang. She remembered lounging against the screen the night before. She remembered the whispers and the secret laughter, and then entering the darkened house. And calling goodnight to Mr. Alston! She thought about that exchange, too. And something else. But whatever the elusive memory was, it disappeared before she'd had a chance to name it.

"Ah, good! The paper's already come!" Henry smiled confidentially to Mabel, and she sparkled back an innocent, "Sorry, Mr. Alston! I should have saved it for you!"

Impervious to other currents in the room, Ruth White sped around the two, setting her Blue Willow ware on the breakfast table as though spreading a meal for a king. The butter dish came out, and the teapot, both sugar bowls (one for lumps and one for plain), the creamer, the dish for the silver tea strainer, jars of marmalade, jam and honey: the list went on.

The kitchen might have been the coziest on earth, and its inhabitants the happiest and most loving to be found.

The teakettle whistled, and the electric toaster sizzled; the hot water tap pluffed sheets of steam while the silverware rattled across the table. To Ruth White, Henry and Mabel, however, these various sounds and smells carried entirely contradictory messages.

"Kippers, Henry?" Ruth White sang. "Wouldn't you like some kippered herrings on toast? I remember the days when you said you couldn't live without them."

This statement was accompanied by a quick wink in Mabel's direction, but the effort missed its mark. Her concentration was elsewhere. In the steam and warmth and comradely haze of the place, she was searching for a friend.

"You're looking awfully nice today, Mr. Alston," she offered with heartfelt awe. "Handsome, I mean. I guess ladies should be nice and men handsome ..."

Henry read a hundred meanings into her words, and his groin stirred with longing and pride.

"Ladies should be nice," Ruth White interrupted with instructive emphasis on the word *should*. "But not all of them are." The private joke caused her to drop a butter knife onto the lead-topped worktable. "Oh, my! I'm at sixes and sevens this morning!"

The innuendo passed unnoticed to all but Ruth White, although she, in her single-minded way, heard the words roll out like the rowdiest talk imaginable. Her face turned scarlet—all the way to the roots of her snow-white hair.

"You're wearing pink," Henry said with his eyes exclusively on Mabel. "I've never seen that dress before."

"It's my special occasion dress. I've been saving it." Her smile was so welcoming and gracious, Henry decided he could have swallowed her whole on the spot.

"I like your yellow sweater set," he said instead. "It's very pretty. On you, I mean."

"Goodness, Henry, the girl can wear what she wants." Ruth White's teasing voice took her husband by surprise. He hadn't said a word to her all morning, had not, in fact, spoken aloud to his wife since the night before. She might as well have been absent from the room, or the house, or the planet, itself.

But Ruth White was impervious; she was adept at carrying on a dual conversation. "She should be thinking about attracting beaus, my dear. I did at her age." Here, Ruth White began a series of sliding trills that were part laughter and part smug self-satisfaction.

Henry paid no heed to his wife's mention of Mabel's possible beau; and neither did Mabel. Perhaps she believed no one in the room knew her secret, or perhaps, removed from the sphere of Jim Flaherty and her own indecisiveness, she momentarily forgot them both. At any event, what she heard was Henry Alston's kindness and nothing more. The gift of his friendship seemed the most marvelous treasure she could own.

"I'm glad you like my sweater. No one's ever told me that before."

If Ruth White had been anywhere else in the house, in the attic or cellar or even the butler's pantry, Henry would have taken Mabel into his arms in a second.

Mrs. Henry Alston was very much alive and present, however, and at the moment she decided to clatter several plates together before rushing them to the table. "Your kippers, dear!" she called.

"Mabel! Come join us! And bring that freshly buttered toast on your way. There's a good girl!"

***

In the Studebaker there was momentary confusion as to the seating arrangements. Henry seemed intent on having Mabel in the front passenger seat; although disappointed at not parading through town at her husband's side, Ruth White was magnanimous in her abdication.

Henry handed Mabel into the front seat first as if he were concerned Ruth White might try to stake a previous claim. In his mind, his wife was relegated to an object as untrustworthy as a wet and sandy dog. He pictured her leaping forward, and forcing her obstinate body in between Mabel and himself.

"You're such a thoughtful person, my dear," Ruth White wanted to murmur in her husband's ear, but she didn't think the gesture seemly. Instead she announced a giddily joyous, "Perhaps Clarissa might take the place of honor when we pick her up!"

Henry decided the afternoon on which Clarissa Tanmere replaced his Mabel would be a cold day in Hell.

***

At Clarissa's apartment house, there was further discussion as to who should sit where. Naturally, she assumed Henry wanted her at his side. Putting *The Vile Girl* there was preposterous—not that Clarissa said as much. Her animosity toward Mabel was disguised under a slash of magenta lips and more of the greasy stuff dotting her teeth.

"Whatever arrangement suits!" she brayed. "I certainly don't want to be the slightest trouble. Back or front, it's all the same to me, although I do so love to watch the countryside through the front windshield of a speeding automobile!"

Ruth White was in agreement with her friend, and Mabel went along with the superior wisdom of both women. She didn't care where she sat; the company of this upstanding and stable group was comfort enough. She felt she'd never been more secure and peaceful in her life.

Henry was adamant, however. "There's far more legroom in back," he advised Clarissa. "Besides being cooler. You know how the sun can heat up the windshield."

Both statements were entirely untrue—facts that did not pass Clarissa unnoticed. She allowed her long body to be wedged into the rear seat, however, and tried to find solace in sitting behind Henry rather than beside him while Ruth White, all temporary generosity, beamed upon the proceedings with the pleasurable smugness of a woman who knows she is truly worshiped.

"Where are we going?" Mabel asked as Henry turned the key in the ignition.

The words possessed an adorableness all too plain to Henry's ears. *Anywhere you wish,* he wanted to murmur, although, of course, he couldn't. In fact, he felt incapable of articulating the slightest sound. He was afraid even a tiny sigh would betray him. Instead, he placed his hand on the gearshift and marveled at his steadiness. Duplicity had become a way of life.

The brief lapse in conversation was immediately filled by both Ruth White and Clarissa. Those self-contained ladies responded with separate though complimentary answers.

"Why, to Miss Tanmere's celebration lunch!" Ruth White squealed while Clarissa boasted a noisy, proud, and faintly argumentative, "The Windsor Haven Hotel, of course!"

Henry was the only person who noticed Mabel quaver at the name, but he excused her hesitation as the natural reaction of sensitive youth when confronted with the preposterous bossiness of age. He yearned to reach out a sheltering arm and protect her from every Ruth White and Clarissa the world could produce.

"You haven't been there, I trust?" Again, Clarissa's tone revealed a definitely combative tone.

"No!" Mabel was quick to throw back. "Should I have?" This time even Henry failed to remark the fear in her voice.

"Oh, my dear!" announced Clarissa with a sound that was the essence of self-serving complacency. "The dining room is the only respectable eatery for miles!"

The word 'respectable' singed through Mabel's brain. Perspiration beaded on her upper lip and her eyes became a terror-struck white. "I haven't been there," she reiterated while Clarissa burst out:

"I should think not!" in a tone intended as jocular, but which fell a long way short. Unkind would have been a better description, or even mean.

On the spot, Henry decided to get Mabel alone as soon as possible. There was so much he needed to say to her, and so many moments and people for which to atone. He grazed her knee with what he hoped resembled a fatherly pat, and the four set off for Windsor Haven.

***

Unwittingly, Clarissa witnessed Henry's gesture, and the motive behind it drove a stake through her heart. *It can't be true*, she told herself. *My Henry can't be besotted with that vixen! That snippet! That unformed calf! That ...!* The more her brain argued, the more feverish she grew. She panted and sweated and waggled her fingers futilely in search of a breeze.

"Do you want me to roll down the window, dear?" Ruth White offered while Clarissa, now waxy and pale, mumbled a pathetic, "Yes!"

"Stop the car, Henry dear!" Ruth White next commanded. "I fear our poor friend is suffering from motion sickness." At that moment, Clarissa, gasping and belching in the rear seat, decided that if the earth didn't open up and devour her soon, she'd find more reliable means of escape.

"Hurry, please!" she whimpered, as much to the fates as to Henry.

***

With the Studebaker pulled to the roadside and settled under a small copse of trees, and with Clarissa and her ministering angel out of sight in the nearby bushes, Henry moved as close to Mabel as he dared.

"I'm sorry about all this," he breathed. "Not a very nice beginning."

"That's all right," she cooed in response. At least, the answer sounded like a coo to Henry's ears.

"We'll do better next time, I promise." Blood flushed his cheeks and neck, making him look younger and ruddier than his years. He also seemed immeasurably strong, or so Mabel, in her yearning, believed.

"That's all right, Mr. Alston. I'm happy to be here, really!" She didn't say anything about their impending arrival at the hotel. Instead, she decided she'd talk to Mr. Alston about her difficulties with Jim. He was kind and understanding. He'd know what to do.

"You can call me Henry," he was about to whisper when Ruth White returned with her ghastly and sweat-stained charge limping behind.

Clarissa smiled weakly, but the blue-white lips and pinched nose gave her long face a skeletal appearance. Despite all pretenses at politeness, everyone averted their faces from the sight.

"And this time my poor, dear friend must sit up front with you, Henry," Ruth White ordered. "A weak constitution like hers. And our honoree, on top of it. I won't hear another word on the subject. My mind is made up and that's that!"

Henry didn't speak. He helped Clarissa ease her rancid body into the front passenger seat. Then he turned to his wife, holding the door open with a cold repose. She misinterpreted his behavior as extreme tact in the face of their new and expanded relationship, and she gave his hand a furtive, suggestive squeeze that he failed to notice.

Mabel, he saved for last. Her pink wool dress rode up on her thighs as she settled into the decidedly smaller rear seat of the Studebaker, and Henry had a glorious, if temporary, view of one of her garter belt clasps, and then a patch of pale skin peeking above a stocking top. His chest thumped; his neck pounded and his shoulders swelled. "There you go," he said in a voice contrived to sound both manly and boyish at the same time.

She repositioned her skirt with a gesture Henry was convinced had been devised for him alone. "Thanks a lot, Mr. Alston."

Clarissa heard every nuance, but her mind was already busy creating a revised and more palatable scenario. *The little hussy!* she railed while the outward manifestation of this fury was an ill-concealed hiccough and unladylike burp. *The ungrateful wretch! Living on Ruth White's kindness, taking the bread from her table, and the very soul from the house! Why, that poor, dear man! He's no match for such shamelessness. That vile, manipulative ...* Epithets she'd only read in books cascaded through her brain.

I'll have to put a stop to her shenanigans. Indeed, I will. I'll watch her like a hawk during luncheon, and tomorrow I'll make my move. Tomorrow when she sets out for classes, I'll waylay her and demand she desist from her evil exploits. I'll make no bones about it! I'll describe everything I've seen. Poor, poor Henry. He's too gentle to withstand such a wicked assault. It's up to me to protect him!

It never occurred to her that Ruth White might be the better person for the job.

***

Luncheon, then. Luncheon in a room whose devotion to the past had filled it with murals of covered bridges, of rushing, trout-filled rivers and sugar maples in full autumnal, red-leafed glory. From the dark beamed ceiling swung pewter lamps, the type that early settlers might have used, and bayberry candles flickered in the room's darkened corners.

High-backed and unpadded settles served as wall-side banquettes while Windsor chairs stretched their stubby legs across the scrubbed oak floor. Dried flower arrangements studded the deep-set windows and sprays of lavender, marjoram, sage and fennel were pinned to the walls as if the restaurant had once been a kitchen. But it was the covered bridges that dominated the scene. Wood-roofed, slat-sided, painted russet or a faded hunter green, their gaunt constructions faced the diner at varying angles. Several structures met the viewer from the side, as though, driving along a country road, the vista had cleared, revealing the passage that lay before. Three were catty-corner, disclosing a shadowy opening to the traveler's eye, while two presented interior views that were the entrance to the span itself.

"Very nice," Mabel murmured although her eyes turned toward the lobby door rather than the room itself.

"I should hope so!" Clarissa retorted as Ruth White burbled a contented, "Shall we?" when the four were led to their table.

***

Under Clarissa's all-seeing eyes, under Ruth White's dreamy perusal and Henry's love-soaked glance, luncheon was served and its courses consumed. Prawn cocktail, lobster bisque, mulligatawny soup, diced carrot salad and corn relish—the food was passed round but scarcely noticed. There were too many violent emotions barreling across the linen-clothed table. Piccalilli, watermelon pickle, calves' liver with onion, swordfish steak, a fricassee of chicken, lamb ragout: everyone smiled and murmured compliments, but the plates might have contained last year's hay.

"Lovely," everyone enthused.

"Simply delicious!"

"I've never tasted such tender liver." Or swordfish, or chicken, or lamb.

Mabel was the only person impervious to the storm circling the foursome, because her thoughts and ears were taken up with worrying over who at the hotel might recognize her face. She tried to smile, but the smile wore thin. She tried to laugh at Henry's jokes, but the laughter cracked. She kept her back to the rest of the room, and her voice lowered and her gaze subdued, and each of these gestures were interpreted by the others according to their personal interests.

Henry saw virginal hesitation. He saw a girl who needed a man's arms and a man's body, a young woman who'd had her first taste of romance and decided she needed something better. He saw every downward glance as a request for his compassion and love, and every flighty glimpse at the lobby door as the stirrings of a lust she was powerless to comprehend or resist. Henry actually imagined Mabel had created a picture of the two of them locked in a forbidden embrace in an upstairs room.

"More butter, Mabel?" he trembled.

"Thanks," she might answer, or, "I'm okay."

In his mind, those simple responses reverberated in their hidden love nest. Clarissa and Ruth White disappeared entirely. He and Mabel had left them behind.

Ruth White watched her husband's extraordinary courtliness and realized she was the luckiest woman alive. Every one of his gestures sent her a secret thrill. She knew the performance was meant for her eyes alone. *If I was a trifle ... inconsiderate of your sensibilities last night ...* he might as well have been nuzzling the speech into her neck, *I do apologize. But my dear, you drive a man to absolute distraction.* The fact that her husband never looked in her direction confirmed her theory. He was overwhelmed with ardor for his wife, and didn't wish to display their love for the unfeeling world.

"Cream for your coffee, Henry?" she asked, and then blushed crimson and pursed her lips.

"I'll have some." Clarissa snatched the pitcher before Ruth White could push it toward her husband's insensate hand. True to her word, Clarissa had kept an eagle eye on the Jezebel seated among them, counting every sigh and eyelash flicker as if adding up sins in a priestly book. In her opinion, Mabel Gorne was damned forever. Bile hadn't help settle the lady's stomach. She tasted liver in her mouth and curry powder and watermelon rind; she yearned for mashed potatoes and cambric tea, egg custard and quiet, but more importantly she longed to have Mabel out of their lives. Dead, if she'd been truthful. Dead, buried, and forgotten. "Ruth White!" she yodeled all of a sudden. "I'm going off to powder my nose! Would you care to join me?"

This was as much of a command as Ruth White had ever heard her friend utter. She started from her chair before she'd had time to consider her actions, then rolled her eyes toward the unseeing Henry as if to say: *You see! You see how much the poor thing depends on me.*

***

In the small and fussily feminine ladies' loo, Clarissa could scarcely conceal her frustration as another guest tidied up, combing her marcelled hair with long and painfully slow flourishes that seemed, in Clarissa's fervid mind, to take all day. She was convinced the foolish woman would never leave, and that she'd never have a moment alone with Ruth White. In order to gain time, she idled at the miniature sink, and then dallied at the rose-clustered mirror, toying with a lavender box of cotton wool before patting a powder puff over her nose. Finally, near despair, she pulled out a handkerchief and buried her nose in a noisy blow that completely eradicated all previous efforts at beautification.

"Ruth White," she croaked when the narrow, paneled door closed at last on the intruder's unwanted back, "I must have a word or two."

The words, spewing forth with ever-increasing friction and speed were these:

"A hussy ... and she's got him in her web. It's as plain as the nose on your face. The girl's the embodiment of evil. I needn't say any more. And, for all the world to see. He's clearly besotted, poor lamb!" Mumbled, vicious, choked, the accusations dashed across the walls, bouncing off the mirrors and the hand towels, off the soap dish and toilet stalls.

"It's been obvious from the beginning ... wanton, I'd call it ... and in your own house, under the very roof that nurtured her!" On and on, the vilifications roared, escalating toward a frenzied crescendo: "Jezebel ... floozy ... trollop ..."

The speech made Ruth White's eyes spin; the mauve-colored paint made her feel dizzy, then faint, then hollow. She reached for a hand towel, dabbed it with water and swiped at her forehead with a gesture as futile as a sleepwalking child's. "And you honestly believe?" she began in a quavering voice, but Clarissa had no intention of forsaking her tirade.

"Well, they say men only wander when they're dissatisfied at home!" Reiterating every hope she'd clung to during her long years as Ruth White's and Henry's unmarried friend, condemnation spewed from her mouth. "Adultery doesn't occur on a happy hearth, my dear."

But this was a fatal approach. Clarissa lost Ruth White's friendship in an instant. The perfectly coiffed scion of the regal White lineage drew herself up until she seemed twice her size. Her expression had turned to ice.

"I'll thank you for keeping your disgusting thoughts to yourself. You are an unmarried woman, and a pathetic one at that. You wouldn't have the slightest notion of what pleases a man! You'd be lost in a male embrace. You'd turn any lover to stone!"

With that, Ruth White banged out of the rose-colored door. She didn't speak Clarissa's name; she doubted she would use it again.

HENRY

The ride home was bumpy, to say the least. Not that Henry minded. The enforced silence that settled within the car allowed him plenty of time to reflect. And reflect he did. With his wife furiously erect at one corner of the rear seat, and Clarissa huddled against the opposite wall, Henry sped across the country lanes, imagining he had only Mabel at his side. Her stillness and quietude puzzled him at first; he'd expected girlish thanks, chatter about what a nice place the Windsor Haven Hotel had seemed, or how she'd like to revisit it one day. In short, he expected delightful innuendo.

Mabel was speechless, however. She stared out the window, and then clenched and unclenched her hands. *She knows something's up,* he told himself over and over. *She knows I understand her feelings. She's biding her time, just as I am.* The only difficulty now presenting itself was the problem of getting her alone. That issue wrestled through his brain all the way back to Clarissa's apartment, all the way through North Chesterfield and finally into the Alstons' drive. *Mabel alone,* he heard the wheels sing. *Mabel alone,* the pavement answered. *Alone with Mabel. I've got to get Mabel alone.*

***

During the night, his salvation appeared. He awoke with a slight headache and a definite grumbling in his stomach. *Lobster bisque,* he told himself, *the stuff's always been too rich for me.* He turned over with a disgruntled sigh, blaming Clarissa and, by extension, Ruth White for forcing the unhealthy meal on him, when he suddenly realized that their feminine demands might just be the cause of his rebirth.

"Sick," he muttered loud enough to lift Ruth White from dreamland. "Stomach ache. Poor Henry's got tummy trouble." In a burst of manipulative brilliance, he shuffled toward the bathroom feigning abdominal agony. Once ensconced in the bath, he didn't bother peeping into Mabel's room. He was much too busy planning his attack.

***

"Isn't my Henums feeling the teensiest bit better this morning?" Ruth White whispered over her husband's closed eyes. Her dressing gown hung at her sides, suggesting neither warmth nor nurturing. There was a mothball smell to its pressed-in folds that somehow never faded from season to season. "Henry dear?" She bent down until the scent of Dr. Lyon's toothpowder merged with the overbearing odor of camphor.

He opened his eyes, as if the effort were the most painful in the world. "Mmmm?"

"Shall I send for the doctor, dear?"

"No. I don't want to disturb him—or you, dear! It's only a bad case of indigestion. It will pass. I only need rest, and to know I'm not troubling you." He believed the great

Alfred Lunt, himself, could learn a thing or two from that dramatic delivery.

"Oh, my dear, you're no trouble. No trouble at all!" She slipped to the foot of the bed, straightening the quilt and rearranging Henry's discarded dressing gown with professional concern. "I'll open the shop, today, dear. I'll attend to everything. Don't you fret. I want you to rest all you can. And Henry." Here her voice dropped to a provocative flutter, "when you're better, when you feel well enough to converse ... well, I want to ... I want us to ... well, you understand ... what we did the other night ... since that time, I've never been able to express ..."

"I understand, dear." He had no idea what his wife was babbling about, but the lie and the comforting tone had become easier than reality.

***

Ruth White was as good as her word. In no time at all, she was dressed and gone from the house, hurrying up the lane to the public bus like a little brown wren protecting her babies.

Henry heard the bus approach; he heard the brakes grind and the metal door crash open, and then the emblem of his redemption drove jauntily toward town.

He was out of his bed in a flash.

***

In the solitude of her bedroom, Mabel heard Henry puttering around in the kitchen. She knew Mrs. Alston wasn't present because of the particularly jarring way in which the dishes rattled and crashed and shook. She decided the mistress of the house must be absent.

The situation seemed odd; she'd never known Ruth White to leave without her husband—or leave her home to a man's devices, but Mabel had begun to realize she didn't know the inmates of the household as well as she'd believed. Take yesterday, for example, and that bizarre escapade between Ruth White and her bosom buddy. A fight had surely transpired, even though neither lady would discuss the situation, or why they'd emerged from their visit to the ladies' room with ill-tempered scowls. And then the trip home in the car! Mr. Alston refusing to acknowledge either woman, and Clarissa alternately trembling and emitting vehement sighs. Mabel remembered having the uncomfortable sensation that the sighs were aimed in her direction, but she couldn't for the life of her imagine what she'd done to offend.

Oh, well, she now decided. *I guess these little jealousies— or whatever you call them—are the natural result of three people living together for too many years. I guess Clarissa envies Ruth White and her nice house and her husband, and maybe Ruth White begrudges Clarissa for not having any of those encumbrances.*

It was this final revelation that drove her down to the kitchen. She needed to share her worries about Jim Flaherty. She needed counsel and the sagacity that comes with age and, although she didn't fully understand her motives, she also desperately needed the guidance of a strong and older male. In her entire, young world, there'd been no one to fill that position. Henry Alston seemed just the ticket.

***

"Isn't Mrs. Alston at home?" She realized the question sounded a trifle sneaky, but she didn't have time to find a paraphrase. She needed to make certain she could talk freely. Ruth White would be mortified at the relationship between an under constable and their "paying guest," whereas Mr. Alston would take the situation in stride. Or so she hoped.

Henry could scarcely contain himself. Here was dream made reality! Mabel, tip-toeing into the kitchen, Mabel querying Ruth White's whereabouts, Mabel conniving to catch him alone! Every one of his fantasies rushed forward with a bang.

"No, she isn't, dear." He put an especially warm emphasis on the word 'dear.' "She'll be gone for the entire day."

"Oh … I see." To his ears, the response sounded relieved—happy almost.

"May I get you some tea? Or would you prefer something more provocative? Coffee, perhaps?"

"Oh, definitely let's share something provocative!" She settled herself in a stool beside the lead-topped table.

Henry's hands remained steady as rocks, and his heart ceased its wild palpitations. He scooped coffee into the percolator top, adding an extra dollop with what he believed was Continental flair. *I have all day,* he reminded himself. *This girl is mine for the taking; I shouldn't rush things; I should take it slow. I must savor every moment.*

"Don't you have class today? Or studies or something?" He needed to hear her motives from her own lips. *Imagine, just imagine if she confesses her desires first!* The possibility seemed better than Heaven, better than sainthood or eternal glory. At that moment, it also appeared remarkably likely.

"Oh, I can skip studying today. Mostly, I can make my own schedule." This was as close to a hint about Jim as she dared. Bringing up her problematic situation wasn't as easy as she'd anticipated, despite Mr. Alston's proffered friendship. All of a sudden, she decided she was letting them both down. She understood the feeling was unreasonable; Mr. Alston didn't have the slightest notion what she wanted to discuss, but the sensation of cheating him as well as herself remained. She compensated with a wide and welcoming smile.

Henry misread the expression. *Oh, the flirt, the little minx! She's going to make me come to her on my hands and knees. Well, two can play this seduction game! And we'll just see who wins in the end.*

"I'm glad you're so free and easy with your time, my dear." He was gratified to see the shadow of a frown pass over his darling's brow.

In answer, she bit her lower lip, and became the picture of dejection.

Henry watched the entire scuffle of emotions cross her face: self-assurance, then consternation, and finally hurt. His heart went out to her; he knew he'd been too harsh.

"Would you like to go for a drive with me?" he begged in apology. "We can take a long jaunt into the countryside. We'll have some privacy there." There was no reason to mention Ruth White. Mabel understood the situation perfectly.

"Oh, yes! Yes, please, Mr. Alston!"

THE WEIGHT OF HISTORY

After that disastrous luncheon, Clarissa also passed a sleepless night, but her wakeful hours had none of the joy of Henry's. Instead, each moment was rife with misery. *Surely, I'm dreaming,* she repeated again and again. *Surely, this is some awful nightmare. Too much piccalilli or mulligatawny soup. I never could tolerate heavy spices.*

But the nightmare was real. With each pained revolution of her blood-shot eyes, she recognized what Ruth White refused to see. *Henry will succumb to the wiles of that floozy, and I'll be powerless to stop him. He'll run off with that bamboozler, and Ruth White and I will be tossed aside like rancid chicken legs!*

"Oh, my dearest Henry! Oh, my love!" The outpouring brought temporary relief. She felt like the heroine of an Italian opera, Violetta, perhaps, the fallen *La traviata* who'd been forced to relinquish her heart's true companion. The comparison to that tragic woman produced renewed sorrow, however.

Her downfall wasn't caused by some fictitious patriarch named Giorgio Germont; it had been created by a very real enemy—the one and only Ruth White. "You wouldn't have the slightest notion of what pleases a man!" Clarissa heard sniggering through her brain. "You'd be lost in a male embrace! You're an unmarried woman and a pathetic one at that!"

She clapped her hands over her ears. "I won't listen! I won't! Ruth White never intended to be cruel. She's been my dearest companion since we were children. She would never wish to be needlessly harsh."

Despite this assertion, the truth began to invade. The fiction of friendship dribbled away. Half-heard words and dismissive gestures rose before Clarissa's eyes: traitorous remarks while still in grade school, betrayals in her teens, teasing, condescension, and finally polite endurance. Everywhere she looked she saw vileness and deception. Except for Henry, of course. *Hadn't he always been chivalrous and good? Even at sixteen and seventeen, when every other boy in the school snickered at her expanding hips and spurting height? Hadn't he always been a perfect gentleman? And long before Ruth White had learned to be a lady. Long, long before.*

"Oh, God!" she cried. "Oh, God, help me!

Self-preservation is an odd thing. It kicks in when least expected. A would-be suicide turns back from the open window because an icy gust serves as a reminder that it's going to be chilly on the way down—and who wants to freeze while falling to death? At this moment in Clarissa's life what saved her was Birdie: Birdie, alive and twittering for all he was worth.

She rose and walked to his cage. "The world's not all cakes and ale. We have to make the best of our lot. We have to soldier on, don't we, my sweet little budgie?"

The words, recited in an orderly fashion, began to work their magic. She smiled. "And now, Birdie, how about a nice piece of lettuce or a healthy chunk of apple? The apples aren't at their peak this time of year, as you know, but never mind, we'll make do! We always have; we always will!"

Birdie chirped, and hopped from perch to perch as if the anticipation of greenery was a thrill too great for his small body to bear.

"I'll put the lettuce on top of Father's armoire and the apple in the curio cabinet. That way you can have your pick. No! Two pieces of apple and three of lettuce, and I won't tell you where to find the other tasty morsels!"

Birdie rushed to the now-open door of his cage, stretched out his green-gold wings and took marvelous flight, lilting and lifting throughout the apartment's three small rooms. He was a flash of brilliance in each corner he touched.

"But mind you keep your eyes peeled for that damn cat! I haven't been myself all night. The wretched creature might have slipped his evil body in here while I was futilely counting sheep."

To demonstrate her warning, she glared at every surface, mimicking the parakeet, stretching her neck and looking sideways from her eyes. "Just make sure! It never pays to take chances."

With Birdie freed to the joyous air, she walked toward the medicine cabinet with the idea of soothing her nerves with an aspirin or perhaps two, but when she opened the mirrored door, she found something better to aid her. "Just a few drops. That's what I gave Father when he was in so much pain. And I'm sure the stuff is still palatable. After all, how can laudanum turn sour?"

She mixed three drops in a glassful of water, and swallowed it with a grimace she needn't have bothered to form. "Why, the stuff tastes like nothing! I can't imagine why Father made such a terrible fuss. But perhaps opiates do fade with the years, after all. I'll take a little more just to be on the safe side."

This time she mixed six drops with a half glass of water, and polished it off with a "There! That's better!"

Relieved from the inner voices that clamored, "Failure! Old maid! Ugly! Unloved and alone," she started to wander her apartment, looking for Birdie. She couldn't see his bright feathers anywhere, but she soon forgot the object of her search. Her brain was growing fuzzy from the drug, although she had no cognizance of disability. Instead, the world seemed rosier, softer-edged; and the problems that had once appeared insurmountable now began arranging themselves into systematic lines.

"I'll write to Henry!" she announced. "I'll send him a note of warning, a clarion call!" The image of herself as Gabriel raising his righteous horn caused her to giggle. Her teeth bucked up and down. She chortled and started singing, "Blow, Gabriel, Blow." The lyrics eased decades of hurt almost miraculously. Cole Porter and his hedonistic realm blew into and through her cramped abode, and she saw herself in the spotlight on a Broadway stage. It didn't matter if the words were out of order, or if her voice quavered. In her mind, she was Ethel Merman, singing for all she was worth.

Still half-singing and half-humming, she took out a sheet of rose-perfumed stationery, an outlandishly feminine purchase she'd never had the courage to use. The Broadway stage disappeared, but she lifted her head as though acknowledging thunderous applause.

Dear Henry, she began, and then crumpled the page into a ball. "Pooh! I can do better than that! Didn't Father always tell me that this earth is not for the faint of heart?"

My dear, dear Henry,

"Oh, Clarissa, where's your gumption, girl? Speak your mind! State your purpose!" She tore up the second attempt.

My dearest Henry,

She studied the letters. There was so much they needed to convey, and the squibs and swirls of ink seemed too paltry a medium. The third sheet of paper fell to the floor. "If nothing is ventured, nothing will be gained." She grabbed a fourth page and plunged the pen into the inkwell:

Dearest love!

I cannot continue like this. Your presence haunts me without ceasing. Your voice echoes in my ear, and your words throb in my heart. I must see you more often—must, must have you to myself, at last. At last, after all these endless years.

Tell me when to come to you, and I will fly on winged feet. And pray, do not fret about the other one, my dear. A woman forgives. A woman always forgives! Consider Lord Byron, if you need examples! Consider Percy Bysshe!

Your own most doting, Clarissa

She believed that mentioning Mabel by name was unnecessary. Henry would understand the person she meant. *Besides*, she decided, *the less I discuss that young trollop, the better. He may realize my womanly wiles are more established than that silly wench's, but one cannot be too careful where men are concerned.*

"I'd turn a lover to stone, would I Ruth White?" she all but hissed. "We'll see about that!"

With those defiant words, she flung the letter into an envelope, bolted from her chair and rushed out of her apartment in order to catch the neighbor's boy, and bribe him into carrying her letter downtown at once. There was no point in waiting for the postman. There was no time like the present!

She didn't care what she looked like; she didn't care how many eyes watched her progress. She paid no attention to her half-buttoned dress, or the gray hair that had tossed off its pins. At that moment, she also failed to notice that she'd left the entrance door ajar.

***

Returning from her mission, Clarissa spotted the open door right away. "Oh, bother." The tone was less than vehement, however. The laudanum was taking charge of her world. "Got to do better next time ..." She shoved the offending door behind her with a lurching crash.

Birdie, in his vegetarian gourmandizing, was disturbed. He fluttered up, all yellow-green terrified wings, but Clarissa failed to notice.

"Birdie? Where's my Birdie?"

By now her speech was turning incoherent. She stumbled toward the medicine cabinet, bumping into every stick of furniture she owned. "'Scuse me ... Sorry ... so sorry ..." The seemingly innocuous word danced around in her head, making her gulp out an hysterical giggle one second and turning her lips cold with grief the next. "Sorry ... I'm so sorry." Even in her drug-induced haze, she realized that it was her life she was apologizing for.

"Always ... Always have been ... sorry mess ... sorry state ... sackcloth and ashes ... sorry I was born." Spinsterhood and years of self-deprivation thrust their way into her mind's eye.

She saw herself and her father: a timid, young girl growing more timorous daily. "You're no better than a mule!" she heard him shout, "and an unattractive one at that! An actress! My stars! You're a Tanmere, unless you've forgotten."

She saw the boys at school, and the girls whose hair and blouses and pinafores always glistened with freshly pressed ribbons. "Mule face! Donkey nose! Clarissa is a sissy! Pudgy, prissy missy!"

Tears began pouring down her cheeks at this last memory. They came in a thick and unconstrained stream, pelting over her cheeks and drenching her neck. "I'll show them! I'll show them who's afraid!"

Blundering toward the bathroom, she bumped against the small nest of Oriental tables and knocked something large and globular from its surface. "Sorry!" she whimpered between her wails. "I'm sorry ... so clumsy."

The round thing hurtled to the floor, landing on four very deft feet, then it dashed under the armoire—a ghost-like gray shape that, to Clarissa's tear-soaked eyes, appeared as cruel as memory.

"Don't," she begged as if the disappearing shape contained the soul of her father, or the taunting boys, or the beautiful, self-satisfied girls. It never occurred to her that the mysterious object was the landlady's cat.

"Please go away," she entreated her ancient enemies as she wobbled unsteadily into the bathroom.

The vial of laudanum was only one quarter full, and she swallowed the liquid with one brief swig. "No good anymore ..."

She never uttered another sound, because at that moment she collapsed, banging her head on the pedestal sink and thudding onto the floor.

Birdie swooped through the door immediately after. He perched on the sink, eyeing his mistress with a sad and quizzical glance, and then flew to the floor, bobbing his bright head up and down as he hopped to her hand and then ascended her arm.

Finally, the truth became evident. Birdie fluttered around Clarissa's head, perching in her ratty hair, and then circling her body like a green-feathered halo or an angel dispatched to earth in order to retrieve the dead.

The landlady's cat was not so sentimental.

HENRY'S STUDEBAKER

At the same hour Clarissa reached for that antique and lethal vial of laudanum, Henry's Studebaker was zipping along a country lane in an area Mabel had never explored. She felt light-hearted and giddy with new-found hope. Having Mr. Alston to confide in would mean she'd never see another problem.

Leaning back in the auto's passenger seat, she watched the leaves flit past the half-open windows, a myriad of lush spring colors: green as shockingly translucent as lime and another as palely innocent as snowdrops pushing upward through a frosting of ice. There were colors, as well— the white-pink of apple blossoms, the lavender of a wild, deserted lilac and here and there something as cherry-bright as hollyhock.

"Where are we going, Mr. Alston?" The tone was only faintly curious. She was comfortable in the Studebaker's passenger seat, comfortable with her present sense of rescue and redemption. Nothing in her history had provided her with the safety she now experienced. "I don't recognize this road at all."

"Call me Henry." He smiled, turning his face toward hers.

The movement caused the wind to ruffle his shock of silver hair, and a wedge of it jolted across his forehead. In the brilliant bombardment of sunlight the hair turned a pewter yellow while the face grew robust and golden. He appeared to have become another man. Even the cut of his jaw became more youthful as the shadows and reflections of clouds and trees molded new and carefree lines, while the light caroming off the car's hood bathed the entire face in a hopeful glow.

"I'll try." She also smiled. "But it's going to be hard." Accepted and appreciated by a person so much older and more clever than she, Mabel sighed with gratitude. Her smile grew.

"Nothing's impossible." He patted her knee in a gesture intended to reassure them both.

"You're so good to me, Mr. ... Henry, I mean ..."

"There's my girl!"

The unwitting appropriation of Jim Flaherty's words brought her worries clanging forward. Memories of herself and her lover flooded in with the breeze: the hotel in Windsor Haven, the afternoons and evenings in his manure-scented car, arguments, hasty resolutions, swallowed secrets in lieu of honesty, one kiss that led to a hundred others—and to the ill-conceived hope that truth would eventually triumph.

She unconsciously slid away from the door and open window, and closer to Henry, as if his sheltering presence could protect her.

His hand squeezed her knee again, and then moved a half inch up her thigh.

"I'm okay, Mister ... Henry... Thanks."

He left his fingers on her leg a moment more. "Anything I can do?"

She should have begun sharing her Jim dilemma then, but the atmosphere was so tranquil she hated to ruin it with chat about a secret beau and her foolishness in allowing herself to become embroiled in such a painful situation. *There's plenty of time*, she told herself. *Plenty of time. And then Mr. Alston will tell me how to extricate myself.*

"No, I'm fine. And very happy to be here."

The car pushed deeper into the Massachusetts country-side. Tobacco sheds and cattle barns, sheep pens and culti-vated fields, the lone farmhouse and the surprising tidiness of a kitchen garden: these were replaced by the scrubby tangle of farmland returned to the wild, and then by the lonesomeness of woodland itself. The trees clustered taller and thicker, and their vine-covered, burly trunks obliter-ated light and air from their lesser companions. An odor of leaf mold and rotting bark, mushroom spores and grubs in hiding rushed through the windows while the view turned dark and creamy as night.

"It looks like no one's ever lived in these parts," she said. "Not even the Indians, I guess. Maybe the place was too spooky for them."

She deserted the right-hand side of the car with a deter-mined wriggle, and settled herself mid-seat. Henry could have easily slid one arm around her shoulder while the other maintained the Studebaker's course.

"I intend to take you to an entirely new terrain," he announced with a worldly nod of his head. "At least, I assume you'll find it so."

***

While Henry and Mabel plunged into the ever-thickening green of the Massachusetts countryside, Ruth White, in the shop on the High Street, was busy setting a box of lead soldiers on top of the counter. The miniature warriors were copied after Teddy Roosevelt's Rough Riders, and she believed they'd been moldering away inside the cabinet far too long.

She smiled and shook her head with doting appraisal. "Just like dear Henry. No business acumen! Why, if he'd arranged a proper display these figures would have sold years ago. What child ever peers into a case when hunting treasures? The objects closest to hand receive attention first—anyone knows that simple rule! And the shinier and more dressed up, the better."

Love suffused her speech. "My Henry ... My dear Henry." The name created a tingling sensation in her breasts that was entirely new, although not unwelcome. "Goodness ... My husband is certainly a naughty influence."

When the Rough Riders were assembled into what Ruth White envisioned as a proper cavalry assault, she peered into the case for some corresponding girls' treat. Lost among a jumbled confusion of hairnets and the paper cards containing bobby pins, hatpins and plain, old-fashioned hairpins was a small comb, brush and mirror set festooned with miniature roses.

The roses climbed the mirror's shiny white handle and dotted the comb's spine and the brush's curved back. They reminded Ruth White of confections emblazoning a wedding cake; they looked too pretty for any activity other than admiration.

She plucked the trio from the display case, and set them on the counter's far end.

"One side for girls, and the other for boys." She was beginning to enjoy her foray into the world of commerce.

From the counter top, she moved to the shop's wall of shelves, peering at the notebooks and jigsaw puzzles, at the bottles of ink and rubber stamps, at the salt and pepper shakers in disguising shapes: fat cooks with aprons and broad smiles or piggies whose curly tails spelled out S or P.

"Goodness. What a plethora of choices Henry has collected. I don't see how anyone could resist!"

***

Telling herself it was now or never, and that she should reveal her secret liaison or suffer the consequences, Mabel watched the world fly past. "Where are we going?" she repeated, but the words were almost inaudible. She sat up straighter in the seat, and swung her feet the way a child would, in order to gain courage for the conversation. Time was running out, and there might not come another opportunity as perfect as this.

A steady and almost jungle-like growth had begun to envelope the automobile. The forest seemed impenetrable; one tree's black trunk half-hid another and then another, a progression that disappeared into dense greenery.

"Have I ever visited this mysterious place before?" An unwelcome apprehension curled around the words, the kind that accompanies tardiness or a sudden wrong-turning.

Although it was generous of Henry to take her for a ride, speech was proving difficult at this breakneck pace. She feared they might return home before she had ample time to talk. "I don't know if we're coming or going, Mr. ... Henry."

"Oh, we're not heading back yet, I promise. I'm taking you to the most wondrous spot I know!" Henry's heart ached as he said the words. He wanted his Mabel in complete accord.

"And where might that be?" The worry in her tone was palpable, but she tried to camouflage it with what she imagined was a quirky turn of phrase—something fun-filled and casual. The most idolized girls at school talked that way, imbuing even mundane speech with overtones that suggested they'd seen and done everything the world had to offer. "This fascinating Shangri-La of yours? Where might we discover it?"

"Mount Tom." Henry knew he couldn't risk saying more at that moment. His vocal cords had thickened with ardor, as had almost every other muscle in his body. He shifted in his seat, and wet his lips with his swollen tongue and then gripped the steering wheel for all he was worth.

"Oh!" The way in which she uttered this innocent sound caused Henry to spin his head in her direction, and his eyes to desert the road entirely.

"You've been there?" Every vision of Mabel now throbbed with a third and villainous presence. In his mind, he became a mere observer, while this girl of his dreams thrashed through the woodsy tangle with another man.

"Oh ... no." She glanced at Henry and his bulging eyes, and then back toward the road. He seemed strangely troubled; she wondered if the cause was age—a "peaky heart" like Ruth White's or any other number of geriatric maladies. She was about to voice her concern, but something held her back, and then planted a seemingly carefree smile on her lips. "I've just heard a lot about the place. I've heard it's pretty spooky. A boy I know told me ..."

The words disappeared in a renewed attempt at off-hand chat. If Henry had asked, "Is there something you wish to confide about this boy?" she doubted she'd be able to take her mind off the pavement and tree limbs and hilly rises skidding by.

But she needn't have worried over his response.

"Getting closer," he murmured as though she hadn't spoken while she quietly begged.

"Aren't we going awfully fast?"

***

At the same moment, ensconced in the cellar of her husband's shop, Ruth White ordered a firm, but merry, "Slow down, my lady! There's no point in rushing the process. You have all day. You can afford to take life at a leisurely pace. Be the woman your husband idolizes. And more. And more. Oh, so much, much more."

These final injunctions caused her to burst into ecstatic giggles. It seemed to her that never in her life had she felt so happy. Not as a little girl growing up as a member of North Chesterfield's oldest and most prominent family, not parading about the village with her beau in tow or entering into the married ladies' conversation as a bride.

Her breasts shivered with another playful twinge, and she experienced some deeper and baser sensation between her legs a second later. "Goodness. Oh my, goodness! What a terrible person you are, Ruth White. You've become quite ... debauched!" It occurred to her that her dear Henry might be experiencing the same wicked pricklings at the same moment, that, lying at home in his sick bed, what he craved above all else in the world was his wife nestled seductively beside him. "My Henums is a naughty, naughty man!" She felt entirely wanton, as manipulative as a lady whose vocation was collecting broken hearts.

Despite this sensation, or perhaps, emboldened by it, she suddenly saw herself transformed and Amazon-like: a woman with male vigor and male resolution. Taking stock of the stored wares, the boxes of shoe and boot polishes that duplicated the ones on the upstairs shelves, the clothes brushes and cedar wood hangers, the bolts of muslin and calico, the mouse and rat traps, the cages for larger marauders, and the tins of poison that irate homeowners demanded when other methods failed, she pictured herself preparing an army for battle.

Then she heard the front door chimes jingle.

The bells, intended to sound joyous and welcoming, shattered her all-omnipotent vision. She dropped a mousetrap as a result of the cacophonous intrusion. The metal clips hadn't been sprung so her thin-soled toes remained safe. Nonetheless, she leapt away from the trap as though a live rodent were struggling there.

"Coming!" she yelled upwards from the depths of the cellar. "I shan't be a moment!" She picked up the mousetrap with some disgust. Although noting the trap was still in pristine condition, with its sanded wood base and copper wire unsullied by rodent hair or blood, she eyed it as if it and not the bell was the cause of her discombobulation. Returning the trap to the shelf, she dislodged a small tin of rat poison, but caught it before it also clattered to the floor. She grimaced with impatience, tightened her fingers around the noxious stuff, and called a loud:

"I won't be a second longer!"

The noise she heard from above the stairs seemed furtive and unsure. She guessed the person was a boy. Footsteps scuttled toward the glass-topped display case. *Oh, the toy soldiers!* she thought. *No wonder Henry keeps the lead models hidden. I should never have been so unwise. My Henry knows better. He always has. And now look where my folly has led us. A thief in my dear husband's shop. A criminal in our midst!*

"You wait right there!"

The boy made no answer, and Ruth White, still clutching the poison, grabbed the stair rail and began to climb the steps. "I'm on my way! You wait right where you are."

It's improbable that a person as petite as Ruth White could have made such a loud, clomping sound ascending the stairs, but she did. The boy, lingering beside the counter top, decided the feet and labored breaths must belong to someone who was very angry.

He took off, racing across the oiled oak floor while Ruth White bellowed, "Come back here, young fellow!" After that, she stood still, quite pleased with the assertive timbre of her voice. "Well! I certainly frightened that young whipper-snapper! Sneaky devil!"

She hurried to her lovingly arranged display. The Rough Riders were still in evidence, still dashing toward some imagined and easily vanquished foe, and the girls' delicate toiletry articles remained in place, as well. She didn't know what to make of the evidence, or lack thereof. Nothing had been disturbed. The picture postcards were untouched, and the souvenir brass tumblers; even the penny candy jar remained unsullied.

Peering through the window, the boy berated himself for allowing an old biddy with white hair to scare him. He lingered, listening, and watching as he pondered whether she'd return to the cellar, and, if so, whether he dared reenter the shop and brave the candy jar—and maybe pinch one of the lead soldiers, too.

Ruth White had no cognizance of being observed. Instead, she brisked about, proud of her courage and fortitude. Then she noticed the poison still gripped in her hand, let out a gasp of dismay, and began retracing her steps toward the cellar stairs. The boy watched, hoping for his chance, but just as she seemed about to descend, she spotted the letter he'd been instructed to leave, and which he'd placed beside the display copy of *The Farmer's Almanac*.

A small yet relieved gasp came from Ruth White. She'd recognized the handwriting instantly. "Why is Clarissa writing Henry?" Setting the poison on the counter and shaking her head in recognition of her one-time friend's numerous quirks, she started reading.

***

By now Henry and Mabel had reached a tourist station at the base of Mount Tom. The one-room, stone building was the starting-off point for day hikers and overnight campers, and it faced out onto a small parking lot, an area filled to capacity during the summer months but that now stood wholly deserted. The facility was empty, too; no ranger was provided until the influx of out-of-state visitors made regulation imperative. The locals knew the mountain trails, and if they didn't, well, they got lost.

Mabel eyed the scene with growing consternation while Henry parked the car, facing it into a tangle of honeysuckle and milkweed, and as far from any late-comers as possible. The dark green paint made the automobile nearly invisible among the brambly vines. Again, she was filled with an unreasonable sense of dread.

He's only trying to keep his car out of the sunlight, she tried to reassure herself. *The light fades the paint; any fool knows that. He's merely being practical.* But the admonitions did no good. Her confession about Jim Flaherty seemed less and less likely to occur in this strange locale.

Reluctantly, she climbed out of the car. Henry didn't help her, which further rattled her nerves.

"Where are we off to?" She wanted her voice to sound cheerily noncommittal, but she wasn't certain the trick worked. To her ears, the cadences seemed tinny and forced.

"Don't you think we should phone Mrs. Alston first? It must be well past noon, and I'm sure she's worried!" She smiled with her prettiest grin, and then smoothed the pleats of her skirt. The gestures were intended to convey self-control. Something told her that calm was required. Mr. Alston seemed odd and self-absorbed. She wondered if he were about to suffer a brain attack. If so, what would she do? There didn't seem to be another person for miles around. She flicked at her skirt pleats again, as if wrinkles were her sole concern.

What Henry received from this behavior were the practiced wiles of a sensuous young woman. The hand drifting over the skirt's gray cloth beckoned him to do likewise while the innocent smile became a salacious leer.

Oh, my darling! he wanted to scream. *There's no need to pretend any further. We're here! We've escaped! We need never go back. We can spend the rest our lives together!* Instead he controlled those impulses, and said in the softest voice he could muster: "My wife won't notice we're gone."

Mabel noticed the sudden insertion of the term 'my wife'; it was a phrase she hadn't heard in a long time. 'My wife'— the words pushed Henry Alston nearer the path of conscientious husband and comforting confidant. She smiled again, this time with genuine confidence. *A nice, slow, private walk. I can reveal everything about Jim now.*

"If you're certain, Mr. ... Henry."

"I am."

Then he led her toward the woods.

***

Ruth White couldn't believe her eyes. "In all my born days!" She put down Clarissa's letter and took it up again. "A snake in my bosom! A viper at my breast!"

The intensity of her wrath increased. She felt as though she were chewing something flinty and tough, something she desperately wanted to spit out. "And my oldest and dearest friend, on top of it! How could any mortal be so craven! After all I've done for her! After all I've put up with!"

She stared into space and then reread the letter. She had a futile belief that she'd find the phrases had been falsified, either by some village miscreant, a library prankster, for instance, or by the room's poor illumination. She held the pages against the light streaming in through the shop windows, and then peered at them under the cash register's lamp.

Clarissa's betrayal didn't vanish, however. Instead, it grew worse with each new perusal. *Your voice echoes in my ear, and your words throb in my heart.*

"How can this be?" Ruth White squeaked. "How can she have bewitched my Henry? How could I have been so blind? Or Henry so treacherous? When did this outrage start?" Memories of Clarissa and Ruth White, of Clarissa and Henry, and then of husband and wife alone crashed into her brain. She saw her friend simpering under Henry's courtly perusal. She witnessed his gentle peck as he returned Clarissa safely to her apartment door. She recalled how the two of them had laughed at some outrageous 'Clarissa folly'—husband and wife, ensconced in their cozy home and life. And she remembered how soothing that shared amusement had been, and how it had suffused her with a sense of worth and superiority.

She watched the remembered years unfold, and all she saw was forbearance on her part and a growing web of intrigue and deceit on the others. *I must see you more often—must, must have you to myself, at last.*

Then she was thrust back into the room she and her husband shared. The time was the previous night. Only the previous night! And Henry was making feverish love to her, a kind she'd never before experienced. "I've got to have you, dearest!" he'd cried out. "I must come to you now!" The memory produced a spasm in her abdomen. Ruth White felt as though rocks were avalanching within her. She gripped the counter top, and nearly crushed the dreadful letter.

Tell me when to come to you, and I will fly on winged feet. And pray, do not fret about the other one, my dear. A woman forgives. A woman always forgives!

"Not always," Ruth White stated. "I don't forgive." Her voice was hushed yet firm. There was nothing in her tone or demeanor that suggested violent emotions at work.

She folded the letter and reinserted it in its envelope, then placed the packet in the cash register drawer, making certain that the handwriting and address were visible. She wanted the person who next opened the drawer to discover the evidence immediately.

"I am not the 'other' one. I am the only one. I am Henry's wife."

At this point, her bravado deserted her. She began to weep. Tears poured from her eyes and lips in a steady, gummy rush. "He's my husband," she sobbed. "Clarissa can't have him!"

She shook her perfect hair, clenched her teeth, and let out a long string of heartrending moans.

"I'll make that damned creature regret her selfish actions. And Henry, too! He's guilty, too, isn't he? Oh … oh … oh …"

All at once, she stopped her spasmodic rocking and stood stock still, grief now supplanted by fury. Casting a malevolent glare throughout the space, her eyes filled with hate and betrayal. "I'll make them wish they'd never been born! Both of them."

With that, Ruth White noticed the discarded tin of poison. She knew precisely what to do.

***

The mountain woods were serene and sun-dappled. Light, the color of honey, rippled downward through the sycamores and oaks and young maples, falling in small and solitary batches that seemed to burn among the leaves.

Mabel walked and Henry walked, and the sound their feet made as they trudged through the underbrush was the snap and crisp of dried twigs breaking beneath their soles and then the swish-swish of fern frond and wild lupine passing around their ankles. Now and then a bird started up, a quail or some other ground-nesting species, but aside from those few fluttered distractions the rest of the hilly path was quiet.

Still unable to address her misguided love life, Mabel had begun concentrating on the airplane lost on the mountainside. She imagined fog as thick as a snow cloud and a pilot flying blind. She pictured the unaware faces of the soldiers inside, the boys returning home from the war; she could almost hear their raucous joy and smell the anticipation beading up on their excited, young faces. The scent was woozy with leather and salt-stained canvas, brass buckles and worn boots; it would have filled the plane's cabin the way the odor of pine boughs floods a house at Christmas time.

"Christmas," she murmured to herself. "They were heading home for the holiday. The war was over. They thought they were safe."

Henry didn't hear her. He was too busy thinking. The mutual seduction he'd envisioned wasn't proceeding as planned. The further they slogged into the woods the more dejected Mabel grew. He had a sense that she was worrying over a private concern, but he had no idea what that problem might be. Time and again, passing some rocky bend in the trail, he expected her to turn to him and declare her love. But she never did. She never looked back or even spoke; she might as well have forgotten he was there.

He started to sweat. Despite the coolness of the spring day, the sky seemed as unrelenting as full summer—full summer and a drought when the sun's rays sap every ounce of moisture from the air. Henry began to feel intolerably thirsty.

But he pushed deeper into the woods and farther up the mountain, zigzagging along the switch-back trail until it seemed that civilization had been totally left behind. Mabel went along, tromping on the dried leaves that hid beneath spring's new growth, and stumbling now and then over some root or twisty vine. He didn't bother to steady her arm, and she never asked for assistance.

Is this the place? she wondered. *Is this where the plane crashed? Was this the spot where the fog cleared and the trees loomed forward and the wings caught fire, and all those on board perished?* She imagined seeing trees where sky should have been; and she pictured the pilot's face, contorted in horror—the only person to comprehend the disaster. "They believed they were safe." Her voice was less than a whisper.

"This is far enough, my dear," Henry said. "This seems like a good spot." He tried to keep his voice on an enthusiastic keel, but the sweat in his eyes and a peculiar wobbling of his knees robbed him of power. He felt dizzy, too, and badly short of breath, although, for once, the cause wasn't Mabel. "I do wish I'd brought us a nice, little picnic."

She turned around, dumbfounded by this statement. She didn't know why Mr. Alston had dragged her to this desolate place, but a picnic luncheon was the farthest thing from her mind. She opened her mouth to speak, but then realized she had nothing to say. Jim Flaherty had all but vanished.

Henry took her wide-eyed stare and parted lips as the encouragement he'd hungered for. "My dear," he whispered. "My dear Mabel."

The name was like ambrosia to his tongue; he believed he'd never tasted anything so sweet. He tried it again. "Mabel ... My Mabel." He might as well have been saying the word for the very first time. "Shhh," he added. "Don't talk. I know what you want to say."

For some reason, she imagined Mr. Alston was about to kill her. She knew the idea was absurd—and that he'd never do anything to harm her, but she couldn't shake the picture loose. She flinched slightly, and Henry took that opportunity to grab her hand.

"Oh, my dear one. Don't you think I understand?"

Here again, her brain deluded her. She tried to tell herself that Mr. Alston meant he understood about Jim, but knew that was impossible. Then her thoughts reverted to the mountain plane wreck, and next to her aunts' house, and the fire engulfing the barn. And finally, to her father. *We're family. First and last.*

Henry lifted Mabel's hand to his lips and kissed it on the palm.

She stared. She didn't cry out, and she didn't pull back. *I know he's very courtly,* she told herself, *Mrs. Alston is always reminding me.* She left her hand in Henry's grasp.

"Dearest!" Lunging toward her, he pinned her shoulders in a clumsy embrace. "There's no need in pretending any more. I know everything. I always have."

Her mind went blank, but her body sprang into action. She slithered out of his arms, and then spun around to face him with her arms thrust forward like a weary fighter.

"We don't have to play this little game any longer, dearest! There's no one for miles. You needn't be shy. We're all alone here. We can do whatever we wish! Whatever you want, darling! Whatever your heart desires!" He made another stumbling grab at the object of his devotion, and this time managed to subdue her arms as well as her fierce, resistant shoulders. Mabel was a tall girl, but Henry was taller and stronger.

"I've watched you, dearest. Every morning. And every night when I could ... I've seen every part of your beautiful body. You needn't be ashamed." He thrust one hand under her sweater and the other up under her skirt. "And I've just waited for the moment when you and I could be alone. I know you want me. You don't have to say a word."

With a sudden, wrenching tug, he had Mabel on her back in the brambly grass. He was on top of her the next moment, flinging her skirt toward her face, and yanking at his trousers' fly with practically the same gesture.

"Darling!" he grunted. "Hold still! Our lovemaking will be so much more pleasurable if you follow my lead."

"No!" She dragged her hands free and pushed them against his chest. But the weight forcing her into the earth was as unyielding as stone. She had a sensation of boulders rolled over her body, as if someone were trying to bury her alive. "Please, Mr. Alston! Please don't do this to me. I thought we were going to talk."

But the more she struggled, the more ardent Henry grew; every time she pulled away, his hands grew rougher and his legs and arms and knees and elbows pushed deeper. She moved her face to one side, but his mouth was on hers before she'd had time to breathe; she slipped a breast out of his reach, but his fingers clutched harder. There was no part of her body he couldn't control.

"You like it this way, do you?" he gasped into her desperate ears. "Your Henry aims to please!" The tone was thick and brutish. The dapper Henry Alston of the suit and shirt and necktie had ceased to exist.

Mabel closed her eyes.

Seeing the shut eyes, and imagining they signaled either boredom or ecstasy, he decided he'd wasted enough time with preliminaries. Mabel was as ready as she'd ever be. He jammed his hand between her legs and tore away her panties.

"Please, Mr. Alston ... I can't ..."

Something in this protest enraged him. "You can't! You can't! You can do it with every other johnnie under the sun, but you can't do it with me?"

Again, practicality deserted her entirely. "I'm not ... This isn't what I thought we'd—"

"Isn't what you thought! You little slut. Coupling with every ruffian in town!" He reared back and raised his hand in the air. When he struck her, it wasn't on the cheek or the jaw or the side of the head or the arm. He hit her full in the chest, crumpling his hand into a fist, and then following the blow with his own determined body.

Mabel lay perfectly still. Her eyes were open, but they neither blinked nor stirred.

Henry Alston rolled around on top of her; he ground his hips into hers. He snatched loose her sweater and pressed his thumbs and forefingers into her waist; he bit her shoulder and slobbered against her tightly held wrists. And he pushed, he pushed. He drove her body upwards through the coarse and scratchy grass, all the while grunting and groaning and swearing and crying.

Her eyelids never fluttered.

When he finally rolled away, she lay inert until she heard him sleeping. And even then, she didn't move. She listened to the sounds of the forest—squirrels skipping through the bracken and birds' feet making monstrous noises in the underbrush—she heard the wind in the pines and another echoing sigh that could have been either an answering breeze or the wail of someone long forgotten. When she was certain he wouldn't follow her, she grabbed up her scattered clothing and ran.

RUTH WHITE DECIDES

With the incriminating letter still clutched on one hand, Ruth White didn't waste a moment. Not that laziness or indecision had ever played a part in her life. Since time immemorial, not one member of the White family had been accused of vacillation or cowardice; and Ruth White, now chained everlastingly to the weak-willed Henry, was the last of her breed.

"We'll have no more of that," she announced. "Such actions cannot be tolerated. What if such people were permitted to breed!" A small sob accompanied these words, but was ruthlessly suppressed. "Just imagine the state of the world if the Henrys and Clarissas had their way!" Her face contorted, as if one half of her psyche were waging war with the other. "They think they're deserving, but they're no better than dirt under my feet!"

She slapped the perfumed note on the shop's countertop, pried open the tin of rat poison, and ladled a healthy amount into a small glass jar. Then she replaced the tin's lid, but found that no amount of twisting could safely reseal it.

Frowning at this unexpected complication, she returned to the cellar and replaced the poison on the highest shelf she could reach. There was no point in inviting casual curiosity. What if that boy were to sneak back into the shop when she was gone? What if he and a friend decided to explore the basement? And what if the two inadvertently discovered the damaged tin and spilled its contents, dusting their mouths or eyes with the stuff? She couldn't imagine how hideous her guilt might be.

"Temptations are better removed from sight." It didn't occur to her that the subject might have been her husband and Clarissa.

With the tin of poison hidden, she left the cellar, stalking up the wooden stairs as though crushing insects underfoot. Gazing around the orderly room, her face turned into a portrait of vengeance; her eyes looked capable of shooting flames. She settled her hat on her head as if she were adjusting a diadem, slipped her fingers into white cotton gloves, and picked up her purse with its murderous contents.

Then she walked out of the shop. She left by the front door. She didn't bother to turn the bolt, nor had she locked the rear entrance. She told herself that closing up in the middle of the day might attract suspicion, but that rationale wasn't honest. Ruth White no longer cared if the place was pilfered; in fact, she wished it would be. She wished every object would be carted off to a more deserving owner than her underhanded husband. If she could have run off in search of the boy who'd brought the fateful letter she would have filled his arms with every lead soldier or model railcar the shop contained. And that would have been just the beginning!

She pictured the child's delighted face, his thrill at the unexpected bounty, the burbled gratitude, the "Gee whiz!",

"Gosh!" and "Golly, Moses" of his inexperienced years; and all at once, her childless state became Henry's fault, as well.

All those years, she almost swore aloud as she crossed the High Street. *All those years when I blamed myself! Spilling his seed elsewhere, that's where his wickedness led him! No wonder there wasn't enough to go around! No wonder my bed was always empty! I never had a proper Christmas because of Henry. I never had a baby to buy gifts for. I couldn't pretend there was a Santa Claus, or read stories at bedtime. No one ever called out 'Mama' in the middle of the night.*

This wrath-filled litany would have continued, but at that moment the bus pulled up, and Ruth White climbed aboard for her journey home. She smiled for the driver's benefit, and then glanced at her fellow passengers to see if any were neighbors or acquaintances. "Warm for May," she offered, although the day was far from hot.

The bus started up, jolting her in her seat and causing her to grab at her hat. One tear rolled out of her eye.

***

Henry wasn't in the house, of course. She hadn't expected him to be, but this further evidence of his cunning only served to enrage her further. Everywhere she looked, every object she touched or idea that flitted across her mind seemed tainted with deception.

"Pretends he's sick!" she all but shouted. "Lies there moaning about 'tummy troubles' while all the while conniving to meet that rotten hag! That miserable sneak who had the temerity, to infer that Mabel was at fault! Poor, sweet innocent Mabel!"

She mounted the stairs at a run. Sure enough, Henry's bed had been left unmade, and its sinfully rumpled state bore witness to the fact that its owner had fled with no time to spare. "Not even the decency to tidy up! Expects me to come home and do the dirty work for him! Well, we'll see about that! We'll just see about that!"

By now some manic being was at work in Ruth White. Her lips were flecked with foamy splotches, and her brow twisted into knife-deep lines that turned a livid scarlet. Even her hair, her perfectly coiffed hair, was transformed. Curls arose where no wave had been, and tendrils started across her neck and cheeks. Medusa and her snakes couldn't have looked more fearsome.

She flew back down the stairs, but not without checking Mabel's room first. True to form, the child had left everything in apple pie order, and there was every indication that she'd been gone the entire day. Her cardigan was missing and the Melton wool jacket she sometimes carried when the weather threatened to turn inclement.

"Oh, to think I could have exposed her to such a man!" Ruth White moaned as she closed the door. "She was like a daughter to me! The child I never had! Why, imagine if she'd discovered Henry's treachery! Imagine if she'd seen him and his harlot friend! What would my baby have thought?"

"My little girl! My dearest hope!" The words crescendoed into a wail, and then were snapped off as though they'd been bitten in two.

***

In the kitchen, Ruth White regained an appearance of outward equanimity. She measured the flour for biscuits, and creamed the sugar and butter together; she broke an egg into a crockery bowl, and stirred the whisk until the white and yolk erupted with froth.

"Oh, Clarissa!" she announced with a playful air, dropping her activities as if they'd been no more than the most trivial of pastimes. "I forgot to call Clarissa and summon her to tea!"

She hurried to the phone, and began spinning the dial with fingers that had turned numb with need. The numbers jumbled together, and she was obliged to begin the process three different times. With each effort her fingers grew colder and the skin more translucent. Veins popped out on the backs of her hand and her nails turned blue.

Finally, the call went through. Ruth White could hear the rings echoing in her former friend's apartment. She recognized the plinking sounds at once, the sad, little 'brr ... ings' and 'brr ... ups' that had always seem the essence of loneliness. Now she realized that wasn't the case.

"I suppose that racket will shake them up a bit!" All the same, she wished Clarissa would answer; it would have been amusing to listen to her squirm for an excuse.

I'll try again, she promised herself. *They've got to climb out of their lovers' bower sometime!*

That thought produced another spurt of activity. She flew around the kitchen, grabbing the preserved ginger and the grater, the cookie sheet and the timer, and then placing every object within easy reach as if she were assembling a bomb. When the sugar and flour and egg and ginger had been blended into biscuit dough, she retrieved her jar of rat poison, setting it neatly beside the crockery bowl.

"Clarissa!" she tittered with a violent giggle. "Time for another call, my girl!"

Again, the phone rang and rang, and the obvious depravity that allowed the call to go unanswered filled Ruth White with a fury so intense she almost knocked the glass jar from the table top.

"Heathens! Immoral hobgoblins!" She pictured her husband and Clarissa rolling about in one others' arms, indulging in the most indecent acts known to man, kissing each other in places too obscene to imagine while they snickered over the poor, deluded wife.

"I'll show them! They won't be laughing for long!" With that, she dumped almost all of the poison into the biscuit dough, and beat the powdery substance until it disappeared. Her fingers flashed through the air, and her wrists turned as angular as pinking shears. Then she scooped half-teaspoons of dough onto the greased cookie sheet, placed it in the oven, set her timer, and dialed Clarissa's number for a third time.

She called a fourth time while the biscuits began cooling on the cookie sheet, and spun the numbers again after transferring her lethal confections to a doily-covered plate. The nearly empty jar of poison she left in a prominent place, but affixed a paper sign "Ruth White Alston's medication for problems affecting the heart. Only for use by Ruth White." She had no intention of allowing Mabel to come to harm.

She tried Clarissa's number a sixth time, but the same hollow tones greeted her ears. The telephone rang and rang but no one raised the receiver from its cradle. Ruth White couldn't see into Clarissa's apartment, of course; she couldn't see the wide, blobby shape sprawled on the bathroom floor or the landlady's cat prowling the inert figure, sniffing the shoulders before stopping to lick yellow-green feathers from under the pads of its paws.

What she envisioned instead was Clarissa's bed (the bed she'd inherited from her sainted father!) and two bodies cavorting beneath the covers. She heard heavy breaths and sighs, gasps of delight and cooing gurgles of wonder.

"That I have lived to see this day!" Her snake-like hair shot out tendrils of rage. "I'm a White. I won't be dismissed or insulted, or betrayed in this shoddy fashion. My family is eminent, and has always been eminent."

At the next moment, the sound of rubber tires scrunched across the gravel drive; she grabbed the biscuit plate and fled into the parlor. She didn't recognize the vehicle's belching groans, but sensed the person might be Mabel. Mabel returning home, with a lift from some total stranger. The thought made Ruth White blanch; she hadn't counted on the girl's presence, and she froze waiting for a youthful "Halloo" to sing out from the rear entrance door.

When no one arrived, she hurried back into the kitchen, listening intently to make certain she was still alone.

***

Tiptoeing into the house on soundless feet, Mabel heard Ruth White at work in the kitchen. She shrank against the front vestibule wall while the familiar smells of baking wafted through the closed panty door. Any second, she expected that Ruth White would call out to her, but no welcome was forthcoming; instead her hostess seemed to be upbraiding someone or something. She even swore!

Mabel thought the behavior peculiar, but she felt too broken to question it. Instead, she wished the Alstons would choke on their Earl Grey and cookies. She wished some awesome evil would befall the couple, and included Clarissa Tanmere in her prayer. Hatred consumed her, and she trembled with helpless spasms while something salty and viscous slithered down her throat, and made her gulp aloud. Her hand flew up to cover her mouth and arrest the noise before Ruth White could hear it. Then she gingerly touched her aching breastbone and bruised jaw. She wondered whether she could ever staunch the pain.

Attempting to steady herself, she stared at the spotless floor and perfectly-positioned runner carpet, but what she saw instead was the hard-packed dirt floor of her Poppa's frame shack, the clodded black earth and the knobby, splayed legs of a table.

She started to cry again, but squelched the sound, and moved toward the stairs. Nothing would permit her to face Ruth White, and nothing in this world could force her to see Henry Alston again. Ever. With her ears attuned to the kitchen, she slowly climbed to the landing, and then to her room. All the while her chest ruptured with hot, dry, and silent wails.

Stop! she told herself as she opened her bedroom door. *Stop at once!* She knew that if her aunts had been present they would have slapped her across the face. And if her Poppa had been—but she didn't want to think about that. *Stop it! Stop or they'll hear you!*

The threat worked. Her body turned motionless; her lips grew cold. It was the first time that she'd remained perfectly still since fleeing Mount Tom. And the first moment in her existence she felt able to view her life as a whole.

In the Alstons' guest bedroom, she stood blinking as if

watching a progression of scenes flit past. One second, she was in her aunts' home, and the next her Poppa's shack. Finally, she saw the journey to Mount Tom. It required effort to convince herself that she was truly safe. She did this by recounting every second of her escape.

Along paths twisted into a wall of tree trunks, snagged at by blackberry thorn and honeysuckle roots, tottering across the edge of a ravine or beneath the grainy faces of perilously-perched boulders, she'd fled through the woods. Down and down, without once looking back. When she'd found the road, she'd loped along it, and then darted into the tangle of sumac, imagining she heard a car's approach.

He's looking for me! kept echoing through her brain. *He'll find me ... He'll find me.* Sinking down on a tree stump, she'd wept. It seemed as if she could never cry enough.

Finally, the sobs had ended, leaving her weak and thirsty and very tired. She thought she might not be able to drag one foot in front of the other, but she had. Trudging along the road, she'd listened for the Studebaker's engine, and categorized every sound and sight and smell she encountered. By the time she'd reached the crossroads that led back to civilization, she believed she knew the hated forest by heart.

***

A truck had picked her up. A truck that had been hauling cows or sheep or pigs. Straw still sailed through its slatted sides, and the odor of the slaughterhouse.

"Where ya goin', girlie?" the driver asked, and she gave the Alstons' address.

"Don't know him," the driver announced. Twangy disapproval pressed against the male pronoun. "But she was a White."

She still is, Mabel nearly corrected, but opted for silence instead.

They rode on without speaking; shards of straw billowed forward at each bump in the road, and the memory of countless suffering beasts wove through the putrid air.

"You one of them Mt. Simmons gals?" the driver demanded at length, and Mabel suddenly realized how torn and tattered her clothing was. She imagined the driver was about to assault her like Mr. Alston had.

"Yes," she gasped through teeth that were prepared for the worst, "I am."

"Got lost up on that damn mountain, did you?" He chuckled, shifting gears.

"Yes." Squinting her eyes, she braced herself, waiting for the truck to stop. Instead, it kept rolling onward.

"Damn place is no good, if you ask me." He followed the observation with an expansive infusion of speech. "My wife says I'm crazy for talking that way. Says someone's gonna come along and lock me up one of these days. Says a place don't have no soul, so it can't commit no evil. D'ya hear about them boys whose plane crashed after the war?"

"Yes."

"Well, there you are. Proves my point. I fought for my country just like them boys. We all did. And those damn Kennedys are fixin' to get us into another war, you mark my words. They're no good, none of them brothers. I don't care where they pretend they're livin'. Sons of Massachusetts, my eye."

Mabel made no response, and the remainder of the journey to the Alstons' house passed in a kind of quiescent amnesty. She believed she'd remember the grind and creak of the truck's gears for the rest of her life.

***

The memories were interrupted as Ruth White banged into the parlor. The noise invaded the upstairs room; even the walls seemed to quake.

"Pretends he's sick! Lies there moaning about 'tummy troubles' while all the while conniving to meet that rotten hag!"

Mabel gasped. She couldn't believe what she was hearing. *How could Ruth White call her a "rotten hag"? Wasn't she the wounded party?*

"Heathens!" Ruth White screeched while she stomped through the parlor. "I'll show them! They won't be laughing for long!"

Mabel steeled herself for trouble. She thought Ruth White was about to fly into her room and accost her. She lowered her head as if preparing to ward off blows.

"Oh, Clarissa! Silly me! I must ask her to tea! We can't let these special biscuits go to waste."

Ruth White ran back into the kitchen, and began spinning the dial. To Mabel, the noise seemed unnaturally loud, as if the instrument were outside her door rather than in the lower floor of the house. She didn't believe a telephone could cause such a cacophony, and wondered whether her ordeal was making her hallucinate.

"I thought that racket would shake them up!" Ruth White slammed down the receiver. "Not answering. She's cleverer than I thought."

Poised between the dresser and her bed, Mabel waited for more disaster to befall her. Body and soul, she yearned to be free of the Alston house, but couldn't bring herself to move. She shut her eyes, but then again saw her Poppa's shack. He was muttering something while he locked the door.

Banishing that image, she opened her eyes, then heard Ruth White dial Clarissa's number again, and scream: "That I have lived to see this day! My dearest friend conniving to woo my husband away from me." Still shouting, she returned to the parlor.

Clarissa? Horse-faced Clarissa? Unconsciously, Mabel touched her bruised breastbone. *What can Ruth White mean?* She kept her hand on her chest, the warmth imbuing a sense of calm, as if it were a kindly person hoping to provide solace. *Clarissa wooing... Clarissa—?*

She had no time for further conjecture, because at that moment, Henry returned, entering by way of the kitchen door, and closing it softly behind him. Acutely aware of the dull plink of wood meeting wood, she was again immobilized by terror. *God no! No, God, please!* She stared at her bedroom door, expecting him to gallop up the stairs and repeat his attack.

Instead, Ruth White's spirited, "Henry! Don't stand there in the kitchen. Come in. Come in." soared upward through the house.

Mabel waited for him to reply, waited for further encouragement from his wife, waited for what seemed like hours on end, and then, finally, decided that she was safe. Neither of the Alstons knew she was in the house. At least, not yet.

Make him go away, her thoughts whispered. *Please. Please.* But the silent plea conjured up more hideous memories, and it took concentrated effort to convince herself that she was in Ruth White's second-floor guest room. Chill consumed her although it was May, not a Midwestern winter.

Shivering, she looked at the white, chenille coverlet that she'd smoothed with such care that morning, drew in one shallow breath after another, and then reached under the bed for her suitcase. After resting it on the folded eiderdown, she began to creep around the room, collecting every stitch of clothing she owned. She didn't want to leave even the smallest trace of herself behind.

TO LOVE AND TO CHERISH

"I've just this minute made a fresh pot of tea—and a plateful of ginger biscuits! By the by, dear, did you bring Clarissa with you?"

Again, Ruth White's voice seemed preternaturally resonant. Mabel winced at its harshness. She didn't recall hearing teatime conversation invade her bedroom, or her hostess assume such a brassy, insistent tone. She scowled, wondering anew if she was inventing this unnatural behavior. For a horrible second, she considered that maybe she was still lost on Mt. Tom, still fleeing from Henry— or worse, still being attacked, and only imagining she'd escaped. *Wasn't that a common phenomenon? Wishing away a disaster? What if I'm still there? What if the truck driver never existed? What if—?*

"No. I didn't see her." Henry had assumed a pugilist's stance, his knees bent between flight and fight.

"Of course not! Of course, you didn't see my dearest friend! What a very silly girl I am! I wonder, dear, if you can ever forgive me!"

Attempting to obliterate the exchange as well as her paralyzing terror, Mabel clamped her jaw. Her breathing hurt, as if every black and blue mark, and red welt, were growing in size. She took more measured breaths, and forced herself to focus on her task.

Into the suitcase went her glass beads, the lacy brassiere, her nightie, and the pink dress of which she had been so proud. She moved with exaggerated care, keeping her footsteps muffled. Even if the Alstons were unaware of her presence, she didn't want them questioning unexpected sounds emanating from the second floor. *Help me*, her brain whimpered. *Help me.*

"Any more tummy troubles?" She heard Ruth White ask. "I was certainly surprised—and pleased—to see that my Henums had gone when I returned. I take it you're feeling better."

"Tummy troubles?"

Recognizing a combination of slyness and incomprehension in his voice, Mabel pictured him in the woods, waking alone with his trousers pushed around his knees, and his shirt torn loose from its buttons, then scrambling to his feet and starting to hunt for her. Her quiet breaths turned panicky. She nearly dropped her pair of dress shoes—the patent leather heels she'd purchased with such care. And at such cost.

"I don't remember any tummy troubles, Ruth White."

"Oh, my dear! Isn't that marvelous! You've already forgotten how ill you were this morning!"

He didn't reply.

Mabel bit her lower lip until it bled.

"I'm certain Clarissa will be here sooner or later," Ruth White announced. "I phoned, of course, but didn't get an answer. They do make her slave away at the library. And dear Mabel must have a late class today. She's usually home by now. I thought I heard her a while back, but I seem to have been mistaken. Why don't we two go ahead without them, and I'll tell you all about my adventures in your shop today."

"Oh God," Henry said in answer. "Oh God, help me!"

Hearing those words, Mabel almost banged her suitcase shut. Instead, she bit her lip again, and tried to continue her packing, but she found her eyes swimming with tears. For a moment, she feared she would vomit. She stood stock still, and prayed the nausea would pass. She wondered why Ruth White made no comment over her husband's inappropriate verbiage, but then decided what the woman did no longer mattered.

"There was a boy who entered the shop while I was in the cellar. At first, I thought he was a thief, but it seems he was acting as a messenger."

"A messenger?"

"Yes. He left you a letter. It's still at the shop. At any rate, the minute I got home from my wifely duties there, I made these for you. And now that you're feeling so fit and full of vigor, we can enjoy a proper feast."

"Ginger biscuits! My favorites!" Even sequestered in her bedroom, Mabel recognized how nervous he was. *Good,* she thought. *Good!* But vengeance went no further. Petite Ruth White would never be able to confront a husband who was so much larger and stronger. Mabel was on her own. Her nausea returned, and with it a sensation of vertigo. *Don't faint,* she told herself. *Don't faint. You're tougher than this. Swallow. Breathe. Ignore them.*

"How kind of you to take such care of me, dear ... dear, little wife."

"Do sit down, dear Henry."

"I think I'll stand, if you don't mind. I feel as though I've been sitting all day."

"And have you? Been sitting all day, that is?"

"Oh, half and half, I suppose. In truth, I've been doing a fair amount of driving."

"Driving! When you're unwell! Well, goodness me. You men are certainly single-minded creatures."

"Of necessity, I should have added."

Mabel glared at the floorboards. She wished she could blot out all sound coming from the parlor, but the quieter and more stealthy her movements, the louder the conversation seemed to become.

"Oh! Then a biscuit is the very thing. I admit that I experimented with these, and would love your opinion, my dear. My dear husband."

In her mind's eye, Mabel watched the scene unfold: innocent Ruth White and her brute of a spouse, playing out their habitual teatime ritual. Were she not so desperate to flee, she might have taken pity on Henry's wife.

"Delicious," he choked out. "These are your best batch to date. Truly! They are perfectly marvelous, dear," he tacked on.

Noting his hesitation, tears of loathing again filled Mabel's eyes. She brushed them aside, and looked out the window at the familiar scene: the neat yard, the one-lane street beyond, a picket fence fronting the neighbor's property, two tidily trimmed boxwood bushes whose acrid scent she had come to associate with serenity. How lovely those sights had once appeared, how comforting, and homey, and filled with optimism. Everything in its place. Everything loving and good and kind.

Then she glanced down at the bed, and heard again Ruth White's gentle corrections upon showing her the room that would house her. "Counterpane or coverlet, dear, not bedspread. And eiderdown, rather than quilt."

Mabel had no cognizance what had conjured that memory, but it produced unexpected grief. "Night stand," she murmured, "torchere lamp ... bed jacket ..." She had never possessed one of those frilly contrivances, and knew she ever would. The notion of lolling in bed while clad in lace and ribbons would have made her smile were she not consumed by sorrow.

Arrested by longing, her gaze returned to the floor.

"My best batch to date, really?" she heard her hostess say. "How kind."

After that, Ruth White remained silent, and, at length, added a subdued: "I do believe I'll keep you company. I'd hoped to wait for Clarissa, but we'll have to make do with each other, won't we? Husband and wife. Till death us do part ..."

Mabel heard something ethereal and unsettling in both tone and words. A frown cut across her brow. This was not the woman she believed she knew. She stared at the floorboards in perplexity. Then her lips tightened, and she grabbed her alarm clock. A gift from her aunts. Staring at the thing, she recalled their injunctions. *"Time with family is a treasure, child. Never forget that. No matter how far you travel. Time with family is sacred.*

She threw the clock into her suitcase.

***

Struggling through her own plight, what Mabel couldn't witness, nor detect, was Ruth White's fateful decision. Taking a biscuit for herself, she paused, weighing the thing in her hand. *So small, and so efficient. A homeowner's perfect convenience—ridding the world of unwelcome pests.* She watched Henry chewing, and the world and her psyche fell into an orderly peace. The energy that had propelled her home from her husband's shop and then set her upon her violent baking spree vanished, and with it her rage and grief.

Maybe this is what death feels like, she thought, *an absence of longing or sorrow or disappointment or pain.* The notion drew her forward ineluctably, as if she were watching all her White ancestors beckoning her. They were clothed in lustrous and silken garments, their faces beaming. "Welcome," they said. "You are welcome to join your own chosen people. We are those who have washed in the Blood of the Lamb, and been purified. Come."

She looked at the biscuit again. It would be so easy to replace it on its pretty plate and allow Henry to fall victim to his own adultery. He would never know what struck him, and she could simply discard the jar with its bogus lettering. No one would suspect her. She'd never even received a detention mark at school. And, as an adult, wasn't she the most model of model citizens?

Instead, she held the confection in her palm and then lifted the pastry to her lips. A smile lit her face, the expression genuine and buoyant. "I think I'll keep you company, Henry. Just as I always have."

The room seemed to spin with the momentousness of her action, and the crowd of angelic beings spun around, as well. She pictured days and months and years whirling past the wainscoting and billowing up into the paneled corners. She saw her mother and her grandmother; she saw Henry as a young swain; she saw herself as a child, and then as a bride robed in antique white.

She saw the twin beds upstairs, and the childless house, watched the sun and rain and snow and sleet shiver along the windowpanes, and Henry venture downtown every day while she arranged pretty pillows or greeted neighbors in the same condescending manner that her grandmother had. Where had been her joy? Where had been her peace?

Ruth White took another biscuit, and then another while the visions continue to dance around her: Clarissa in pig-tails sucking her thumb, herself as a girl practicing scales on the piano while outside a sultry August breeze stirred up the voices of ball-playing boys and an enticing aroma of dust.

***

Of these regrets and misspent passions, Mabel hadn't the slightest ken. Soundlessly, she had continued stripping the room of her belongings. Notebooks, socks, pencils, underpants, and a worn eraser: all lay jumbled into a haphazard mound within her suitcase—her "portmanteau"—while Ruth White repeated a melancholy:

"In sickness and in health."

The tone brought Mabel to a standstill. *What does she have to mourn? She, who's as naïve as the day she was born? She's never known anything but this town, and a life*

*of complacency. And purity, too. I'll bet her father was some
upstanding citizen. And her mother, too.* All at once, Mabel's
fury turned on her supposed friend and guide. *She should
have protected me. She should never have accepted me as a
boarder. She should have understood that her husband ...
She should have—*

The silent rant ceased when Henry answered:

"Those fine, old vows, Ruth White. Your memory's a
wonder. In sickness and in health ... For richer, for poorer
... To love and to cherish."

Batting aside his loathsome voice, her disgust at the
craven Ruth White, as well as recurring bouts of terror,
Mabel forced herself to finish her task.

"I think I'll treat myself to another. Henry?"

"I've had sufficient, dear."

"Oh, I insist! Let's finish the whole batch!"

"Anything to oblige."

"That's right. You and Clarissa would do the world for me,
wouldn't you?"

"No need to ask that question."

***

Promising herself she would never, ever be forced to hear
another word from Ruth White or Henry Alston, Mabel
closed her suitcase, secured its clasps, and crept from the
room in her stocking feet. On the landing, she paused. The
parlor's inhabitants had ceased their conversation, but she
waited, believing it would start up again, as it always had.

The silence continued. At length, she felt compelled to
move lest her good fortune change. Hefting her battered
case, she hugged it close to her body so as to avoid hitting
the stairs' risers or banister and arousing suspicion. The

other hand held her shoes, scuffed and grass-stained from her race down the mountain.

After descending the front stairs, step by slow step, she tiptoed along the hall, through the butler's pantry, and entered the kitchen. Her heart pounded, expecting Henry to loom into sight at any moment. She held the suitcase handle tighter, promising herself that the heavy case would make an excellent weapon. She almost wished she could use it.

The residents of the parlor remained mute, however. Or, perhaps, she'd finally found the ability to silence or ignore them. She allowed herself the glimmer of a smile. A sense of inner power burgeoned. She felt equal to the treachery of the Ruth Whites of this world, if not yet from the Henry Alstons.

After pausing another second, she crossed to the telephone, and started dialing Jim Flaherty's number, but before she could complete the call a clatter burst through the pantry door. With the phone still cradled in her hand, she heard china cups rattle with a shattering plink, silver teaspoons smashing into the sugar tongs, and then spilling, as if thrown, across the floor. Finally, the tray itself, the large, oval Sheffield tray that was Ruth White's pride and joy dove downward in an echoing heap. The sound reverberated like a thunderclap.

Expecting words of recrimination or apology or consternation over the mishap, she froze, again overcome with fear. *I was so close,* she told herself. *So close to an escape.*

Clinging to the receiver, she gazed at the kitchen as if seeing it for the first time. *Why had she never noticed the room's similarities to her aunts'? Yes, the metal screens in the door and windows weren't sagging and patched, but the coppery color was the same, as were the chrome legs of the stepstool. As to the sink, oh, it was a mirror image. How had she failed to recognize the parallels? Or was this another form of hallucination?* Mabel saw herself wrist deep in soapsuds in both places, and lost all sense of the present.

Trying to dislodge both the near and distant pasts, she shook her head, and fingered her aching breastbone with her left hand. She attempted to eradicate all memory of Henry Alston: the rasp of his voice, the stink of his body, the ferocious grip of his hands. But her mind pictured him lurching through the pantry door and into the kitchen. She didn't dare turn her head, for fear the inventions would turn into reality.

Then, without warning, she remembered her father looming over her, too. He was drunk, but his steps were steady. Striding forward, he looked as invincible as a giant. "There's a good girlie," he'd slurred just before the shack's locked door burst open and her aunts rushed inside, cursing her and wailing. *Was one of them armed with a broom?* Mabel tried but couldn't recall, although she could hear their fierce cries, and see their white aprons stretched taut over their ferocious, flailing forms. She had lowered her head and closed her eyes while her aunts sprang into action.

She opened them now.

Loyalty is a gift from God clanged into her thoughts, and then a muted: *Ruth White was like a mother to me.* Like a miracle, her aunts and father disappeared.

***

The dull beep of a failed connection brought her back into the present. Mabel stared at the receiver as if she'd forgotten why she'd picked it up in the first place. She didn't remember noticing the words Western Electric on its underside, but they produced a thin, bitter smile. She was tempted to toss the thing onto the floor.

Instead, she gazed at the telephone, and made a decision. All at once, it seemed so natural and self-evident. Irrefutable, really. She smiled in earnest and lifted her jaw, then returned the receiver to its cradle and coiled the ropy cord beside it.

Gripping her suitcase in one hand and her shoes in the other, Mabel walked out.

AFTERWORD

The idea for *They Believed They Were Safe* came to me in a dream. I admit that I'm given to vivid and often violent dreams, and that snippets of them make their way into my novels. When I'm in deep author mode, I feel that I'm channeling my characters, and my dreams—or nightmares—are theirs, rather than my own.

I also envision segments of human existences whenever I pass abandoned buildings or drive on roadways where houses once stood. I hear voices and often abbreviated conversations. Am I inventing them, or am I intuiting? I have no answer, but readers of my other works of fiction know that I'm most comfortable—perhaps, happiest—when exploring historical eras.

They Believed They Were Safe was different from any of my previous dream experiences. Mabel Gorne, Ruth White, Henry Alston, Clarissa, and Jim appeared fully formed. Each possessed a name and complex history. Nothing as comprehensive as this had ever occurred before. As their stories unfolded, my sleeping self became increasingly perturbed. I forced myself to waken, then walked around the house attempting to rid myself of their grim chronicles.

Convinced that I'd succeeded in banishing the tale, I returned to bed, but drifting back to sleep found that they were waiting for me. It was as if each character had perched on a section of the mattress, demanding to continue the narrative. They were in a terrible rush to proceed. I was unable to prevent them from doing so.

As someone who is addicted to historical research, I have hunted for possible references to this tragic story, but found nothing.

So, did Mabel Gorne, et al live and struggle and die in a small New England college town in the early 1960s or did I fabricate the tale? Or is some greater narrative working through them?

ACKNOWLEDGEMENTS

Thank you to my husband and fellow novelist, Steve Zettler, who believed in *They Believed They Were Safe* since page one and who felt that Vine Leaves Press would make a fine home for the work. Thanks to dear friend and scrivener, Merry Jones, for an early and comprehensive reading, as well as a great deal of encouragement.

And special gratitude to my editor, Melanie Faith, for her guidance, queries, enthusiasm, and perspicacity. *They Believed They Were Safe* is a deeper and richer novel due to her insights. VLP is fortunate to have you. So am I.

A final shout out to Jessica Bell and Amie McCracken who have built a fine and discerning publishing house.

Gratitude, also, to Dan Hart for the coiffure.

OTHER BOOKS BY THIS AUTHOR

Sins of Commission
The Actress
Without Fear
Deception's Daughter
The Conjurer
Beneath the Wind

Biddle, Jackson, And A Nation In Turmoil
Saint Katharine: The Life of Katharine Drexel

VINE LEAVES PRESS

Enjoyed this book?
Go to *vineleavespress.com* to find more.
Subscribe to our newsletter: